William – The Rebel

Just – William a facsimile of the first (1922) edition
Just William as seen on TV
More Just William as seen on TV
William at War
Just William at Christmas
Just William Through the Ages
The Woman Behind William: a life of Richmal Crompton
by Mary Cadogan
School is a Waste of Time!
by William Brown (and Richm...

"I'LL TELL YOU IF YOU PROMISE NOT TO TELL ANYONE,"
SAID WILLIAM.

(See page 226)

William—The Rebel

RICHMAL CROMPTON

Illustrated by Thomas Henry

MACMILLAN CHILDREN'S BOOKS

First published 1933

First published in this edition 1985 by
Macmillan Children's Books
Reprinted 1995 by Macmillan Children's Books
A division of Macmillan Publishers Limited
London and Basingstoke
Associated companies throughout the world

4 6 8 10 9 7 5

ISBN: 0-333-38908-5

A CIP catalogue record for this book is
available from the British Library

Phototypeset by Wyvern Typesetting Ltd, Bristol
Printed and bound in Great Britain by
Mackays of Chatham PLC, Chatham, Kent

Contents

William invites you!

*Join my club and becum a nOutlaw
William Brown*

You can join the Outlaws Club!

You will receive
a special Outlaws wallet containing
your own Outlaws badge
the Club Rules
and
a letter from William giving you
the secret password

To join, send a postal order for £2.50 and a letter
telling us you want to join the Outlaws, with your
name and address written in block capitals, to:

**The Outlaws Club
Macmillan Children's Books
25 Eccleston Place
London SW1W 9NF**

You must live in the United Kingdom or the
Republic of Ireland in order to join.

Chapter 1

Three Dogs and William

The whole trouble, of course, began with Ethel. Ethel had never had a dog, and there didn't seem to be any reason why Ethel should have a dog. She didn't like dogs. She didn't understand dogs. She had never felt that all-consuming urge to own a dog that assists in replenishing the coffers of the State. She disliked William's dog, Jumble, intensely, and regularly accused it of the destruction of any of her personal articles that she happened to have lost or mislaid. She was afraid of big dogs, and she said that little dogs made her feel sick. . . .

When William heard, therefore, that Ethel was going to keep a dog he felt both surprised and indignant. Further investigation proved this decision to be the result of one of Ethel's bewilderingly swift affairs. A youth in the neighbourhood, who had conceived an ardent attachment for her, had, as a mark of that attachment, asked her to take charge of his Alsatian while he went on a holiday abroad. He had originally arranged for his sister to do this, but, having met Ethel and fallen beneath the spell of her blue eyes and red-gold hair, he had hastily cancelled the arrangement and given his pet into Ethel's charge, hoping thereby to bind her affection to him more deeply. Ethel was touched and gratified. She had lately been to see a film in which the heroine had possessed an Alsatian and had posed with it very effectively in a baronial hall and on the terrace steps of a large and park-like garden. Ethel's home had no baronial hall, its garden was devoid of terrace or steps, but she meant to reproduce the poses as best she could, and even improve on them. The young man, who evidently took the Alsatian (its name was Wotan) very seriously, gave her a long list of duties in connection with it. It had to be brushed and combed and cleaned and dosed and fed and exercised with alarming frequency. Moreover, it had to be exhibited at the local dog show, which was to take place in a week's time.

"He's a dead cert for a first prize," said the young man earnestly. "He'll want to be got ready properly, of course. I've just written down the few things I generally do to him before a show."

And he handed Ethel another long list of preparations. She felt depressed for a moment, but the young man had a straight nose and a nice smile, and she longed to try some of the poses that the girl on the pictures had used so effectively. Having seen that film, she would always now feel incomplete as a pretty girl without an Alsatian.

"Oh, I shall *love* to have him," she said brightly. "I *adore* dogs, you know."

It wasn't till the Alsatian had taken up his quarters in the house and the young man had actually set off for his holiday that Ethel realised the complications that would ensue from the meeting of Wotan and Jumble as dwellers on the same hearth-stone. She had always looked upon Jumble as beneath contempt. She had imagined that Jumble would realise his inferiority in comparison with the noble Wotan and behave accordingly. But Jumble didn't seem to realise anything of the sort. Instead of welcoming the new guest with grateful obsequiousness, he greeted him with open hostility, snarling and growling and gathering himself together for an attack.

He was immediately ejected from the room, and William was ordered to keep him, in future, out of the new-comer's way.

"I like that," William muttered indignantly. "Yes, I *do* like that. Who came here first, I'd like to know—Jumble, or that Wotan thing? Rotten he ought to be called. Well, I don't think it's fair. Jumble's got a *right* to his own home, hasn't he? S'pose someone came an' turned *you* out of your home an' said someone else must come in. How'd *you* like it?"

But Mrs. Brown supported Ethel. Mrs. Brown, too, was impressed by the aristocratic appearance of the Alsatian. Moreover, she always upheld the law of primogeniture.

"Ethel's the elder, William," she said, "so if the dogs can't live peaceably together then yours must go out of the house. Jumble's got his kennel and, anyway, he's never in the house much."

"He's in when I'm in," said William fiercely, "and it's his *home* an' he's had it all these years an' then you go an' turn him out for a rotten old thing that looks more like a donkey than a dog, anyway."

His mother, however, remained adamant, and Ethel was deaf to all his insults. She was enjoying the novelty of possessing a dog, and was combing and brushing and cleaning the creature with commendable assiduity. Moreover, she was practising the poses. It was, she found, more difficult to enter a room with one hand laid negligently on Wotan's head than anyone would have supposed. He had a way of suddenly withdrawing or hurrying forward at the psychological moment in a manner that completely spoilt the picture.

Still, she persevered, and certainly Wotan looked

majestic and picturesque pacing by her side. William showed his displeasure by absenting himself completely from the house except for meals and sleep.

"If it's too good for Jumble," he said coldly, "it's too good for me. I don't want to stay in a place that's too good for Jumble. An' let me tell *you*, Jumble jolly well doesn't *want* to come into the house, so there! Not while that ole Rotten's here, anyway."

Jumble's behaviour, however, belied this statement. Jumble most decidedly did want to come into the house. Jumble knew that the house contained a rival and a foe, and he barked and growled defiance at it all day long, tugging at his lead when William led him past the door, straining at the kennel chain and snarling savagely when Ethel strolled past, her hand laid negligently on her new friend's head after the manner of the film heroine. Wotan ignored his presence, merely throwing a glance of haughty contempt in his direction as he passed. He seemed to look on Jumble as a creature with whom he could have no possible dealings. But there came a time of disillusionment and reckoning. For one afternoon Ethel sallied forth with her attendant hound without seeing first that Jumble was fastened up, and Jumble hurled himself upon the majestic Alsatian with the pent-up fury of many days. The Alsatian had evidently conceived a deeper dislike of Jumble than he had allowed to appear in his demeanour. He returned the attack with interest, snapping with such vigour that, when the dogs were finally separated by William and the gardener, Jumble had to be taken to the vet to have his side stitched up. The vet decided to keep Jumble for a few days. He had had much past experience of William's amateur surgery.

William returned home dogless and disconsolate. Ethel, of course, said that it was entirely Jumble's fault.

"Wotan didn't do a *thing* to Jumble till Jumble flew at him."

"Oh, didn't he!" said William bitterly. "Well, let me tell you it was *all* that ole Rotten's fault. How would *you* like to be turned out of your house and have someone else carrying on as if it belonged to them? I suppose *you'd* jus' sit quiet in a kennel an' do nothin'! Huh!"

He tried to annoy the majestic Wotan by pulling faces at him or making provocative noises, but Wotan ignored him completely. Wotan was now the pampered darling of the household. Ethel scented his hair and tied blue ribbon round his neck. Mr. Brown bought him an indiarubber bone as a plaything, but Wotan sniffed at it disdainfully, then turned away. Wotan was not the type of dog that plays with indiarubber bones. . . .

* * *

William walked slowly and desolately along the road. Each Jumble-less day seemed like a month to him. Jumble led an adventurous life, and it was not the first time that he had had to retire for a few days into the vet's charge. It was not that that gave the situation its peculiar bitterness. It was the sight of Jumble's rival and assailant in possession of the house and garden that William looked upon as belonging by right to his own pet.

He slouched along, his hands in his pockets, his toes dragging in the dust.

"That ole Rotten!" he muttered disconsolately. "Huh! Hung for murder, that's what he ought to be, 'stead of havin' indiarubber bones an' suchlike given him!"

He turned round to gaze with deep self-pity at the empty space at his heels where Jumble normally trotted along behind him, then stood still in amazement. A small white dog was trotting along behind him. It wasn't

Jumble. It was smaller, rougher, even more suggestive of a mongrel than Jumble, but it trotted at William's heels as if it belonged to him; it stopped when he stopped, and wagged its tail, gazing trustfully up at his face.

"Good old chap!" said William, and the little white dog curvetted ecstatically about his feet. William began to walk on again and, glancing carelessly over his shoulder, was much gratified to find that the little white

THE SMALL WHITE DOG GAVE A LOW GROWL, AND SPRANG UPON THE ASTONISHED WOTAN.

dog still followed. He pretended to himself that Wotan did not exist, and that he and Jumble were walking home together after a morning's rabbiting in the wood. This mental picture, however, was rudely shattered by reality, for at a bend of the road there appeared Ethel, walking slowly along with Wotan, one hand resting on

THE BATTLE WAS SHORT AND INGLORIOUS. IN LESS THAN A MINUTE WOTAN WAS FLEEING DOWN THE ROAD.

his head in painstaking imitation of the pose. She looked disappointed to find that the turn of the road revealed no other spectator than William. As William approached he fixed a deliberately contemptuous gaze upon the lordly Wotan.

"Huh!" he muttered scornfully as he came abreast with them.

Suddenly all was pandemonium. The small white dog, evidently mistaking William's contemptuous "Huh!" for a new form of "Sick him!" gave a low growl and sprang forthwith upon the astonished Wotan. The battle was short and inglorious, and in less than a minute Wotan was fleeing down the road, pursued by a small white tornado. A torn and trampled blue ribbon was left to mark the battle-field. Ethel, who had screamed hysterically while the fray was going on, now snatched up the trampled blue ribbon and ran off, still screaming, after her pet. William stood and watched with a smile of quiet enjoyment. . . .

Soon the little white dog reappeared, running back along the road. He was obviously very much pleased both with himself and William. He leapt joyfully up at William, then took his place again at his heels, trotting demurely along.

Life had now taken on a new aspect for William. All his dejection had left him. He had a dog, a super dog, a dog who could turn the noble and majestic Wotan into a fleeing streak of lightning. Life was worth living again, gloriously, hilariously worth living.

He swaggered up to the front gate, his new friend still trotting trustingly at his heels. Mrs. Brown was there waiting for him.

"William," she said, "it's very unkind of you to set strange dogs on to Wotan like this. It's upset Ethel very much."

"I didn't set a strange dog on it," said William. "I didn't set any dog on it. My dog was jus' trying to have a game with it, but that ole Rotten's such a coward."

"Your dog?" said Mrs. Brown. "But Jumble's at the vet's. . . ."

Then suddenly she saw the little white dog looking up at her, wagging its tail ingratiatingly.

"William!" she said, dismayed. "*Whatever's* this?"

"That?" said William carelessly. "That's my new dog."

"You *can't* have another dog, William," said Mrs. Brown firmly, "you've got one."

"Well, it's at the vet's, an' I want a dog to be going on with. I want two, anyway. If Ethel can have one as big as that ole Rotten I ought to have about six ordinary size ones to make up."

"Well, you can't, William," said Mrs. Brown. "I'm absolutely *sick* of dogs," she added fervently, "and I'm dreading the time when Jumble comes back to make more trouble. You musn't *dream* of keeping this dog."

"I'm not keeping it," said William, astutely changing his point of attack. "I can't stop it following me, can I? I've done all I can to stop it following me an' it isn't any good, so I'll jus' have to put up with it."

"You can't keep it, William," said his mother firmly. "I'll go and ring up the police now, and see if a dog's been lost."

Rather to her disappointment, it turned out that no dog had been lost. Mrs. Brown asked the police to come and fetch the dog, but the police politely refused to do this. She had apparently given the dog shelter, and therefore she was responsible. If she sent the animal in question to the police station they would receive it, but they would not come to fetch it.

"You can take it to the police station or get rid of it

some other way, William," said Mrs. Brown; "but I simply won't have it here."

Thoughtfully William walked away, followed happily, trustingly, by his new friend. Half an hour later he returned alone, wearing his famous expression of imbecile virtue.

"I've got rid of it," he said.

"Did you take it to the police station?" asked his mother.

"No. I got rid of it on the way," said William. "I thought that was the best thing to do. I jus' got it lost on the way."

"I am very glad you did, dear," said Mrs. Brown, much relieved, and gave him a large piece of cake, which he took to the old barn and shared with the little white dog who was tied up in the farthest corner of it.

The little white dog seemed to take quite happily to his new existence. During the day he roamed the fields and woods with William, staying in the old barn when William had to go home for meals, and spending the night in the tumble-down summer-house that no one ever used at the bottom of the Browns' garden. He seemed to thrive on the odd mixture of scraps, purloined from the Browns' larder, that now formed his staple diet. One would have thought that he had never known any other existence than this, any other master than William. William discovered that, though docile and friendly ordinarily, he turned into a little tempest of ferocity when "sicked" on to fight. He had the courage of a dog twice his size—and a brave dog at that. William longed to bring about a decisive combat between Wotan and his new pet, but to advertise his new pet's existence in this way would be to secure his final dismissal.

The day of the show was drawing near, and Ethel was intent upon the preparations for it. Wotan was brushed, combed, cleaned, dosed and dieted with renewed energy. He was given a tonic to steady his nerves for the ordeal. He slept on a specially prepared bed, raised from the ground in order not to expose his precious person to draughts. A new length of blue ribbon was bought for him. William suspected that Ethel's heart was not in these preparations although she carried them out so conscientiously. The novelty of possessing an Alsatian was wearing off. She had been again to the pictures and seen a film whose heroine played with a kitten in a way that made the only two possible poses with Wotan seem extremely dull. Moreover, the memory of Wotan's owner was growing dim, and she had now met another young man—with an even straighter nose and nicer smile than Wotan's owner's—who wasn't interested in dogs. Still—she was intensely anxious for the kudos of Wotan's victory. She felt that she would be dishonoured for ever if Wotan failed to win his first prize.

The day of the show arrived. Wotan, brushed, combed, sleek and shining, his neck adorned by an enormous length of brand-new ribbon, was led out by Ethel into the back garden. Ethel wore a new hat and looked rather nervous.

"Jus' stay there a minute, sweetie 'ickle man," she said, "while mummie goes to fetch a keen hanky."

Despite her affectionate tone of voice she looked at him rather coldly. There was something very unresponsive about Wotan. She had never really been able to establish contact with him. A kitten would be much more satisfactory in every way.

She had no idea, of course, that that little scene had an audience. William happened to be passing the house with his white dog and, as always, was skirting it furtively by way of the field that bordered the back garden, so as not to expose his pet to the eyes of his unsuspecting

family. Through the hedge the two of them were
watching with interest the final preparation of Wotan.
Ethel gave the blue ribbon a final tweak.

"Doesn't he look a pretty ickle boykins!" she said,
laying her cheek against his head.

Wotan continued to gaze blankly into space.

Ethel sighed wistfully and went indoors. Wotan continued to gaze into space. The sight of him sitting there in

THROUGH THE HEDGE THE TWO OF THEM WERE WATCHING WITH
INTEREST THE FINAL PREPARATION OF WOTAN.

sole possession of the garden from which he had ousted both Jumble and the little white dog, the smugness and conceit and stupidity of the expression with which he gazed around it, were more than William could endure.

Before he realised what he was doing he had whispered a quiet, low "S'k." The small white tornado shot through the hedge and flung itself upon the nonchalant giant. The giant, dropping his nonchalance, put

"DOESN'T HE LOOK A PRETTY ICKLE BOYKINS!" SAID ETHEL, LAYING HER CHEEK AGAINST HIS HEAD.

up a fairly good fight, but he was no match for the white tornado. He fled yelping round and round the garden, pursued by his valiant little foe. Once more his blue ribbon was torn and trampled. One ear hung bleeding. There was a deep scratch down one flank. In his wild efforts to escape he knocked over a watering-can of water and rolled over on the rose-bed. Gone was his perfumed elegance. . . . He was muddy, dirty, and bleeding—no object for a dog show or indeed for a public appearance of any sort. Ethel, drawn by the growls and snarls, came running into the garden. William called off his pet, but not before Ethel had seen it. They hastily departed, leaving Ethel moaning over her fallen hero.

William did not come home that night till bedtime. Ethel had gone to bed in a state of nervous collapse. Wotan sat on the dining-room hearth-rug, wearing his bandages with an air of mournful pride. William was at once taxed, as he knew he would be, on the subject of the little white dog. He had prepared an attitude of complete innocence that sounded less convincing than he had hoped it would sound.

"That dog? Which dog? Oh, yes, I remember. That dog that followed me some days ago. Well, I told you, didn't I? I lost it. I lost it when I was takin' it to the police station. Yes . . . now you mention it, I *do* think I've seen it about once or twice since. Yes, I have seen it about . . . but I can't help that, can I? I can't stop dogs walkin' about in the world if they want to, can I? Was it that dog that went for ole Rotten? I'm not sure whether it was or not . . . yes, I happened to be jus' in the field an'—yes, now you mention it, I did see a dog go for ole Rotten, but how can *I* tell whether it was that dog what followed me an' what I lost? I don't know every dog in the world, do I? I don't see how I can, consid'rin' there mus' be thousands an' thousands of them.

"Anyway, it isn't anythin' to do with me, is it, if that ole Rotten can't stick up for himself? . . . I tell you I don't know what white dog it was. I only jus' happened to see a white dog goin' for him. I keep tellin' you I don't know all the white dogs in the world. . . ."

But he was aware that he did not deceive them. As he went to bed he decided that until their suspicions were lulled he must find some other night's lodging for the little white dog than the summer-house. He woke very early next morning and at once went to look out of the window. To his horror and amazement he saw a man in leggings, carrying a gun, walking towards the summer-house. He recognised him as the gamekeeper from the Hall. He realised at once what had happened. His father had discovered the dog in the summer-house last night and, urged on by Ethel, had asked the gamekeeper to come round and shoot it first thing in the morning. Without stopping even to put on his slippers, William hurled himself downstairs and into the garden. He next proceeded to hurl himself upon the gamekeeper. The gamekeeper, however, was not attempting to shoot anything, for the simple reason that there was nothing to be shot. The summer-house was empty. William stared at it in surprise. Only last night he had safely secured his pet in it. He must have got out through the window that William always left open for ventilation. At that moment there came sudden signs of consternation from the house. The housemaid had come down to find the silver gone and signs everywhere of the recent presence of a burglar. A scream from Ethel proclaimed that her jewellery had gone. Meantime, the lordly Wotan slept peacefully upon his patent raised bed. The gamekeeper searched the bushes and outhouse, prepared to shoot small white dogs and burglars indiscriminately. Mr.

Brown, clad in his pyjamas and armed with a poker, rang up the police. . . . Gradually quiet ensued, and the family went to dress.

In the middle of breakfast there came a telephone call from the police. The burglar had been found with the spoils upon him. He had evidently been tracked and was being held at bay by a small white dog. The small white dog was keeping him in one spot, snapping at him ferociously whenever he attempted to move, and barking loudly to attract attention. Two policemen brought the spoils back to the Browns' house. At their heels trotted proudly the small white dog.

"*Well*," said William, "surely now he's saved all your lives and the silver *and* Ethel's pearls—surely you'll let me keep him *now*."

But Mr. Brown was reading out an advertisement from the morning paper. "Lost, probably in neighbourhood of Marleigh, small white dog, answering to the name of Tinker. Reward offered."

As one man the Brown family rose and went to the open window, outside which sat the little dog, gazing up expectantly.

"Tinker!" said the Brown family simultaneously. There was no doubt as to the little white dog's response. He hurled himself up at the window with every sign of ecstasy.

Mr. Brown at once got into communication with the telephone number given in the advertisement and was informed that the advertiser would come at once, arriving early in the afternoon.

The various members of the family spent the intervening hours in various ways.

Ethel spent it taking Wotan to his owner's sister.

"I'm afraid I can't look after him any longer," she said sweetly. "I simply *adore* him, but I'm just simply too busy to look after him any longer. Yes, I'm so sorry about the show yesterday. He had a fight and couldn't be shown. Yes, it was very unfortunate."

She left Wotan sitting on the drawing-room hearthrug, still staring majestically in front of him, and went down to Marleigh to enquire the price of kittens . . . playful kittens . . . the sort the girl on the pictures had had. . . .

William spent the morning in sorrowful company with the little white dog. Its charms seemed to multiply as the hour of its departure drew near. William didn't know how he was going to part with it. . . .

Mrs. Brown spent the morning removing the traces of the burglar's feet from the hall linoleum and his fingermarks from the furniture.

Early in the afternoon a young man arrived. He and the little white dog greeted each other with rapture.

"I'd sooner have lost anything in the world than this fellow," said the young man, holding the little white dog affectionately in his arms. "I brought him back with me from Africa. He's the world's best hunting dog. He can hold up a lion or a leopard anywhere—keep out of his way, but simply hold him to the same spot, just as if he'd got him tied up. He's a pretty valuable little chap, too. There aren't many of his breed about. I was motoring with him past here on my way to London last week, and I suppose he must have fallen or jumped out from the back of the car. I'm jolly glad to see him again, I can tell you. Let me see . . . who actually found him?"

William, of course, had actually found him, so the young man gave William a five-pound note. This was little compensation to William for the loss of the little white dog. In any case five pounds was too large a sum to be of any use to William. It would, he knew, be confiscated by his father and put to swell his post office savings account—a procedure that William regarded as a shameless, deliberate swindle.

Ethel's blue eyes and red-gold hair were having their wonted effect upon the young man.

"I'm awfully grateful to you for being so good to my little chap," he said fervently.

"Oh, I *adored* him," said Ethel, fluttering her tawny lashes entrancingly; "we *all* adored him. We shall miss him horribly."

"I can see you're a dog lover all right," said the young man, his admiration deepening.

"I adore dogs," said Ethel unblushingly, as she mentally relinquished the playful kitten in favour of a small white dog.

"Of course, most people think he's a mongrel," said the young man.

"Oh, I knew at *once* that he wasn't a mongrel," Ethel assured him.

William exchanged a slow wink with the little white dog.

The young man had driven off at last with his dog, after arranging to call and take Ethel out for a drive one day next week.

William was left alone to consider the situation. The house was clear of Wotan—that was one good thing. But it was also clear of his little white friend, which was not so good. Still . . . William could not help seeing that there were redeeming factors in the situation. He would insist on having at least five shillings of his five pounds in hand. And—he felt relieved that Jumble's courage was no longer under a cloud, as he had secretly felt it to be ever since he had been so ingloriously chewed up by Wotan. After all—you couldn't expect Jumble to be just like a dog trained to "bay" lions and leopards. No, Jumble was certainly as brave as any ordinary dog possibly could be. His affection rushed out towards his faithful pet, who had gone through so many adventures with him. He wondered how he could possibly have lived all this week without him. He wondered how he could possibly have thought that even the little white dog could take his place. He suddenly remembered that the vet had said Jumble might be able to come home to-day.

Whistling loudly and untunefully, he set off down the road at a run towards the vet's home.

Chapter 2

A Rescue Party

"What I think's so awful," said William, seated firmly on one of his favourite hobby-horses, "is that I've lived all these years and not *done* anything yet."

"You've done quite enough," said his mother. "You've broken every window in the house at one time or another, you've made the geyser explode twice, you've *ruined* the parquet by sliding on it, and you've got tar all over the hall carpet."

"Well, I can't help them putting tar on the roads, can I?" said William, stung by the injustice of this accusation. "I've got to walk somewhere, haven't I? I can't fly, can I? It's not fair to blame *me* because people put tar on the roads. Besides, I didn't mean that sort of thing, anyway. I meant the sort of thing that makes you famous. The sort of thing people put up statues to you for, I meant, it's awful to think of me living all these years an' not done anythin' yet to make the world ring with my name."

"The world'll ring with your name all right," said William's elder brother, who had entered the room in the middle of William's diatribe. "I bet you any money we'll all live to see you hanged."

William ignored this remark except for a withering glance of which he was secretly rather proud.

"What I mean is," he continued to his mother, "that with wastin' all my time in school like what I have to, I

never have any left to do anythin' to make the world ring
with my name. I bet I'd've been famous by now if I
hadn't had to waste all my time in school."

"One might almost say you're famous now," put in
Robert, who had remained unwithered by William's
withering glance. "At least, everyone for miles around
knows there's some sort of trouble coming as soon as he
sees you. I suppose that's fame in a way."

"What could you have done, dear?" said Mrs. Brown
hastily to William, seeing him preparing to meet this
challenge.

"I'd have invented something," he said, his attention
drawn once more to his wrongs. "Look at all the things
that've been invented by other people while I've been
wastin' my time in school. I did invent somethin' to stop
Mrs. Bott's chimney smokin', but there must've been
somethin' wrong with the chimney. The *invention* was
all right. Or I'd have caught crim'nals. I bet I'd be jolly
good catching crim'nals, only I never get a chance to try.
I bet I'd've had a statue put up to me for catchin'
crim'nals by now if I'd not had to waste all my time in
school."

At this moment Mrs. Bott was announced, and
Robert made a hasty exit. William stayed behind, not
because he derived any pleasure from Mrs. Bott's
society, but because he wished to continue his conversation with his mother as soon as the visitor should have
departed. He had thought of a lot of exploits by which he
might have made his name famous if he had not been
forced to waste the precious hours of his youth in school.
He might have discovered a new continent. He might
have tamed a jungle full of lions. He might even have got
into communication with Mars. . . .

"I bet there'd have been hundreds of statues up to me
all over the world by now," he muttered indignantly.

"What do you say, dear?" said Mrs. Bott, who was slightly deaf.

"Nothin'," said William morosely.

His mother glanced at him apprehensively.

"Don't you want to go out and play, William?" she said.

"No, thanks," said William.

"Hadn't you better be getting on with your homework, then?" said Mrs. Brown, who had no wish to resume the unending discussion on the uselessness of school. It was a perennial source of contention and each knew the other's arguments by heart.

"Homework!" echoed William and uttered a hollow laugh.

Mrs. Bott looked at him with interest.

"I think he needs a dose, dear," she said to Mrs. Brown. "I believe in Gregory powder myself. It's old-fashioned, I know, but there's nothing like it for these bilious attacks."

William threw her a glance before which—in his imaginary exploits—strong men had quailed. Mrs. Bott met it unflinchingly.

"Bilious," she said with deepening interest to Mrs. Brown; "you can see it in every line of his face."

Without a word William walked slowly and majestically out of the room. But he lingered in the hall within earshot in case they should begin to discuss him. They didn't, however, somewhat to his disappointment. Instead Mrs. Bott said:

"I was going to ask you to come to tea with me next week, dear. Botty's gone up to Scotland for a little holiday, and I'm that lonely . . . "

William walked abruptly away. He wasn't interested in Mr. Bott (always alluded to by his wife as Botty), the short, stout manufacturer of Bott's Sauce, who lived at the Hall, and whose generosity compensated in the eyes of the neighbourhood for his lack of education and his frequent omission of the letter H.

He wasn't interested in Mr. Bott, and he wasn't interested in Mrs. Bott—large, florid, golden-haired, vulgar and good-natured. He was only interested in himself and his frustrated fame.

"Eleven years old," he muttered bitterly to the umbrella stand, "and not done a *thing* with my life but sums an' g'ography an' stuff like that."

Then quite suddenly he made up his mind. He'd run away and seek his fortune. Not a minute more of his life must be wasted. He'd set out now this minute. Before him lay the world, holding at every turn innumerable promises of fame and fortune. He'd walk to the sea, keeping an eye open for adventures on the way, of course, and there he'd join a band of pirates. He'd make himself master of the pirates and discover a new continent, then, having conquered the natives, he'd make himself king. After that he'd train his conquered natives till they were the finest army in the world and then there wasn't any reason why he shouldn't conquer the whole world. All this would take time, of course, and he hadn't a moment to lose.

The first immediate necessity was provisions for his journey. Cautiously he entered the larder and, finding a pile of meat pasties on a plate there, crammed as many into his pockets as they would hold. These simple preparations completed, he put on his cap and set off jauntily down the road. Rather to his disappointment he reached Marleigh, three miles distant, without adventure. Outside Marleigh he sat down and, though it was only a short time since he had had his tea, ate the meat pasties. He meant to eat one only, but somehow he had finished them before he realised it. One had broken into

**WILLIAM CRAMMED AS MANY INTO HIS POCKETS AS THEY WOULD
HOLD.**

tiny pieces in his pocket, but William was no whit
disconcerted by this. He ate every fragment, including a
piece of string, some bits of crayon, a small piece of
rubber, and a generous sprinkling of ants' eggs, a packet
of which, destined for his goldfish, had lately broken in

his pocket. Cheered and refreshed by this mixed diet, he set off once more. He did not know the country beyond Marleigh, and he went slowly and warily, as a man might go in a lion-infested jungle. He would be disappointed to meet with no adventure before he reached the sea. A cow stared at him mournfully over a hedge, and he returned its gaze suspiciously, as if it might turn out after all to be some wild animal in disguise. But it remained indubitably a cow, and William walked on, depressed and disappointed by the ordinariness of life. Suddenly he brightened. . . . A high wall ran along the roadside, and behind the wall, some distance from the road, William could see the chimneys of a large house. He looked up to the top of the wall. A row of broken glass bottles embedded in cement crowned it. . . . The sinister aspect of this struck William at once. Here was his adventure ready to hand. He must find out what nefarious design was being hatched behind this grim fortification and bring the perpetrators to justice. That surely would give him fame. . . . It would probably indeed lead to the offer of a high appointment at Scotland Yard. William decided to accept the appointment when it was offered to him. . . .

He wandered round the wall till he came to a small wooden gate. He tried it, and to his delight it yielded. He entered a picturesque kitchen garden. Seeing two gardeners at work on a vegetable bed in the distance, he crept cautiously along by the inside of the wall till he came to a yew hedge that separated the kitchen garden from the garden proper. He squeezed through this with a certain amount of difficulty, deciding *en route* that the taste of a yew hedge was inferior to the taste of hawthorn, privet, or beech (William was a connoisseur in the taste of hedges), and found himself on a spacious lawn. The house was now revealed to him—large,

square, ivy-covered. Its largeness and squareness gave it
a satisfactorily sinister and prison-like appearance.
There was a line of shrubs at the side of the lawn, and
under cover of this William made his cautious way to the
house, then began very warily to peep into the windows.
The first room he inspected was a handsomely appointed
drawing-room, the second a handsomely appointed
dining-room, the next a kitchen. . . . William hurried
past this. He had learnt by experience that the
inhabitants of the kitchen are apt to be particularly
unceremonious in the treatment of small boys found
loitering on the premises. The next room was a small
study, in which a man sat writing at a table. William
thought that he had the look of a man who was head of a
gang. . . . He walked on to the window of the next
room, then stood, paralysed with amazement, eyes and
mouth wide open. For there on a table, clad only in his
vest and pants, lay Mr. Bott—Mr. Bott, who was
supposed to be in Scotland! And that was not all. For a
tall, grim-looking man in a white coat was engaged in
savagely pulling Mr. Bott's arms and legs, first an arm
and then a leg, in a way that was obviously designed to
force them out of their sockets. At each jerk Mr. Bott
screwed up his face in agony.

"Torcher!" said William to himself, with mingled
horror and satisfaction. "They've captured him on his
way to Scotland, and now they're torcherin' him. . . ."

He would have liked to watch longer, but a sense of
personal danger made him reluctantly tear himself
away.

He returned to the road, and there stood still for a
moment to consider the situation. There was no need
now to run away to sea. Here was fame ready to hand.
By freeing Mr. Bott from the nest of kidnappers and
torturers, by exposing and bringing to justice the whole

gang of them, surely he would become so celebrated that Scotland Yard would ask him to lend them his services. He decided that he would only lend them on condition that he was made one of the Big Five.

He was aware, of course, that the situation must be carefully handled. To begin with, he wasn't going to let the police in on it. They would take all the credit to themselves. On further consideration he decided not to let any grown-up in on it. Grown-ups were notoriously ungrateful. If there were any credit to be got out of the *coup*, they would get it themselves and pretend that he'd not done anything. He uttered a scornful laugh. Huh! He knew grown-ups by this time. . . . They'd do all they could to keep him out of the Big Five. He walked homewards thoughtfully. The difficulties of the situation seemed to increase as he pondered on them. He had, of course, more than once discovered what he thought were gangs of criminals, but subsequent events had proved that his imagination played a rather too large part in the affair. Always the "criminals" he had discovered had turned out to be ordinary law-abiding citizens. But this was different. He had with his own ears heard Mrs. Bott declare that her husband had gone to Scotland. He had with his own eyes seen Mr. Bott not five miles from his own home, being manhandled by his captor in a large, prison-like house. . . . There could be no possible mistake this time. But he must go carefully. Though he had no small opinion of his own physical and mental powers, he realised that he must have assistance of some sort to manage the affair successfully. He decided to consult his Outlaws. They might be able to help him evolve some plan.

He went slowly to the old barn which was his head-quarters, and where he was more likely to find his Outlaws than anywhere else. He found them, accompanied by a large crowd of their schoolmates, playing "French and English". Left to themselves, the Outlaws had very little imagination in the matter of games. At first William was disconcerted not to find them alone, then he brightened, realising the possibilities of the situation. He would take all these boys with him to rescue Mr. Bott. Though small, they would surely by sheer numbers overpower the jailer in the white coat and release the prisoner. . . . Moreover, unlike grownups, they would not try to steal the credit from him. He was their accepted leader. They were accustomed to follow him. Already he felt himself a general leading his troops to victory.

Ginger greeted him somewhat shamefacedly, aware that "French and English" was not quite worthy of his powers of invention.

"Hello," he said; "you weren't here and there didn't seem anything else to play at. . . ."

"I'm going to make a speech," said William, dragging out of the old barn the packing-case that usually formed his rostrum. Ginger, assuming his usual function of William's aide-de-camp, made a funnel with his two hands, and shouted: "William's going to make a speech."

The boys stopped playing and crowded round the packing-case, repeating the shout: "William's going to make a speech."

William mounted his precarious stand.

"Ladies and gentlemen," he began. There were no ladies present, but William always considered that the correct opening for a speech in all circumstances. "Ladies and gentlemen . . ."

This opening was conscientiously applauded by his followers, and, clearing his throat, he continued:

"You've all gotter come an' rescue someone—

someone what's in prison havin' his arms an' legs pulled
out what his wife thought was in Scotland all the time.
Well, how would you like your arms an' legs pulled out
when your wife thought you were in Scotland? What I
mean to say is that when we find people pullin' other
people's arms an' legs out we oughter *stop* it. It's an
unkind thing to do, an' we oughtn't to do unkind things
like the good Samaritan in the Bible. I bet if you go with
me to where this man is—havin' his arms an' legs pulled
out by a man in a white coat—we'll jolly well rescue him
an' stop people in white coats pullin' other people's
arms an' legs out, 'cause it's a very wrong thing to do.
Pullin' arms an' legs out is forbidden by lor. I'm goin' to
Scotland Yard when we've done this rescue an' I'll give
any of you a job as a policeman when you're old enough.
You can't have quite such a high-up job as mine. Stands
to reason you can't, 'cause it was me what found this
man in the white coat pullin' his arms an' legs out, an'
it's me what's goin' to take you to rescue this man what's
arms an' legs are bein' pulled out."

He paused for breath, and thunderous applause broke
out. They were not quite sure what it was all about. They
were clear only on one point, and that was that William
was going to lead them to adventure. They were heartily
tired of "French and English", and welcomed any
change. Gratified by the reception of his speech, William continued with rising eloquence:

"What we've gotter think of is this: Would we like our
own arms an' legs pulled out by a man in a white coat?
An' if we wouldn't, then—"

Further speech was drowned by a large report as the
packing-case gave way beneath him, precipitating him
among the *débris*.

But there was no need for him to continue. Already
the rescuers were eagerly preparing themselves for

battle, seizing even upon the fragments of his erstwhile platform as weapons, and brandishing them above their heads. He crept out from the *débris*, removed a nail from his hair, a piece of wood from his mouth, and several splinters from his hands. He then examined his knees with interest.

"I bet I'm goin' to have a bruise as big as a football on this knee," he said. "Well, that *shows*, doesn't it?" he continued, turning the episode skilfully to account. "If jus' fallin' off a box hurts as much as this, what mus' it hurt like to have your arms an' legs pulled out? . . . Well, who's coming to this place where they capture people goin' to Scotland an' pull their arms an' legs out?"

They were all coming apparently. Already Ginger was marshalling the band. Already miniature battles were taking place with pieces of packing-case as weapons.

"Come on, then," said William, slipping one hand inside his jacket in faithful imitation of the picture of Napolean that formed the frontispiece of his history book. "Come on. We don't want to find him with no arms or legs left when we get there. . . ."

Eagerly the band set off. One boy produced a whistle from his pocket and blew it lustily as he walked. Another ran into his house, which they passed on the way, and came out with a tin tray, which he beat jubilantly with a stick.

William, however, sternly forbade these exuberant manifestations of the martial spirit. "D'you want them to *know* we're coming?" he said indignantly. "D'you want to give them the alarm so's they'll clear off to the Cont'nent with him an' when we get there we'll jus' find an empty house? Haven't you got any *sense*?"

The crestfallen musicians meekly put aside their instruments and walked on in (comparative) silence.

Outside the wooden gate in the high brick wall William addressed them again in sibilant tones, his collar turned up with fine conspiratorial effect, and wearing the tense frown of one who engages upon a desperate undertaking.

"Now, listen," he said. "This man's imprisoned here by a gang what captured him when he was going to Scotland. They're torcherin' him in here, pullin' his arms an' legs out, an' what we've gotter do is rescue him. Give me that whistle."

The owner of the whistle meekly gave it to him.

"Now you come with me to a hedge here, an' I'll go an' scout to find out where he is, an' then when I whistle you mus' all run out and rescue him. . . ."

Fortunately for the band of rescuers, the kitchen garden was empty. Following William, they crept through to the cover of the yew hedge and there William again addressed them in the sibilant whisper.

"Now you stay here an' wait," he said, "an' I'll go'n' scout, an' remember when I whistle all run out an' rescue him."

He crept along the edge of the lawn till he reached a copper beech, beneath which a garden roller made a convenient step. In less than a minute he had swung himself up from the roller into the branches and had crept along the lowest one as far as he dared, in order to keep his look out upon the house and garden. At present there was nothing of interest to see in either. The garden was empty. The downstairs rooms were empty. . . . Then suddenly Mr. Bott came out of the house and began to wander about the garden. He looked morose and miserable. He heaved deep sighs as he walked. . . . William formed his plans quickly. He would wait till Mr. Bott reached the spot just beneath his branch. Then he would blow his whistle, drop down, and with his band of rescuers rush the prisoner to the door in the wall and thence homeward. Mr. Bott paced slowly on towards the tree. He came beneath William's branch. William blew his whistle and dropped. The drop was only partially successful. He had meant to land just in front of Mr. Bott. Instead he landed on the top of Mr. Bott. The two of them rolled on to the ground, Mr. Bott struggling violently and shouting: "Help, help! Murder! Fire! Thieves!" The band of rescuers leapt upon him, pulling him, pushing him, dragging him by his coat, hustling him from all sides.

"Help, help!" shouted Mr. Bott again. "I'm being murdered!"

"Shut up," ordered William fiercely. "Can't you see you're being *rescued*? Shut up an' come on. We're *rescuin'* you, I tell you."

Mr. Bott, however, continued to struggle with his rescuers, and soon the man in the white coat was seen running across the lawn from the house. During the *mêlée* that followed William came to the conclusion that his opinion of the physical prowess of his contemporaries had been unduly optimistic. The noble band of rescuers was scattered by a few well-aimed blows from the new-comer's fists and a few well-aimed kicks from his boots. They fled in panic before him, pushing each other from behind in their eagerness to reach the wooden door.

"And if you come in here again with your monkey tricks," shouted the man, "I'll wring your necks—every one of you."

"Huh!" said William, picking himself up from the road where his hasty exit had landed him. "Yes, I bet he'd wring our necks all right. . . . Well, doesn't that *prove* he's a torcherer like what I said? Who'll come back an' try again?"

But nobody wanted to do that. The rescuers had had their fill of rescuing—for the present, at any rate. They had enjoyed the adventure on the whole, but, as an adventure, it was now perfect and complete. To add to it in any way would be to gild the lily. So they marched back, blowing the whistle and beating the tray to their hearts' content.

"I bet we'll have scared him," said Ginger. "I bet he'll let him go now. I bet we've jolly well rescued him."

The rescuers enthusiastically adopted this attitude as one that satisfied honour and exempted them from again encountering the fists and boots of the man in the white coat.

"We've rescued him," they chanted to the accompaniment of the whistle and the tin tray; "we've jolly well rescued him."

William felt less sure on this point. But he realised that some other method must now be tried. He had over-estimated the intelligence of Mr. Bott (who had not even the sense to recognise rescuers when he saw them) and underestimated the physical prowess of the white-coated torturer. For a few minutes he was at a loss. Then his face cleared. The wronged wife, unaware that her husband was in the hands of kidnappers and torturers . . . She would surely feel enough gratitude to one who discovered the plot to see that he received his due reward. Mrs. Bott, though devoid of most of the graces conferred by breeding and education, was generous to a fault. She was, moreover, touchingly, childishly credulous. She would not pooh-pooh his story as most grown-ups would, and so waste valuable time and give the villains opportunity to escape. He dismissed his hilarious band (still blowing the whistle and beating the tray) and set out purposefully for the Hall.

A disapproving butler opened the door. Mrs. Bott's

butler had once butlered a duke and despised all Mrs. Bott's visitors on principle, but there was more than his normal disapproval in his eye when it fell upon William.

William, indeed, fresh from his exploit of attempted rescue, was not a reassuring sight. His hair stood on end, his collar was burst open, his tie hung under one ear. He was covered with garden soil where a blow from the man in the white coat had landed him neatly into the shrubbery. Laurel leaves adorned his hair.

In fact, Mrs. Bott's butler's indignation was such that he found it difficult to retain the official calm upon which he prided himself. To have sunk to Trade was bad enough, but to have such objects presenting themselves upon one's front door-step . . . He closed his eyes and a spasm of pain passed over his chiselled features.

"Do you know where the back door is?" he said in a hollow voice, opening his eyes, only to close them again with another spasm.

"Yes," said William in unsuspecting friendliness. "'Course I do. Have you got lost? I'll show you if you like. But I want to see Mrs. Bott first."

"Mrs. Bott?" said the butler in a faint, suffering voice.

"Yes," said William, pushing his way unceremoniously into the hall.

"Have you an appointment?" said the butler, gathering his scattered forces.

"Lots," said William, putting on a careless swagger in order to hide his ignorance of the meaning of the word.

Wincing, the butler collected a few laurel leaves from William's hair and dropped them with ostentatious disdain on the front door-step.

"Don't you bother about me," said William, touched by this attention. "I don't mind a few leaves an' things about me. Is she in the drawing-room?"

"Mrs. Bott is not at liberty," said the butler.

"Yes, she is," said William; "it's *him* what isn't. That's what I've come about. Where is she?"

"I've already told you—" began the butler.

"Well, I can't stop here chattering with you like this," said William kindly. "I'm busy."

He pushed past the butler and made his way into the drawing-room.

Mrs. Bott was lying on the sofa, reading a novel. She looked up as William entered and gazed at his dishevelled figure in alarm.

"Whatever mischief have you been in now, William?" she said. "I never saw such a sight as you look. I am sorry for your poor mother. I am reelly."

"He's bein' torchered," said William abruptly.

"What?" gasped Mrs. Bott.

"He's bein' torchered," repeated William. "He's having his arms an' legs pulled out."

"Now, William," said Mrs. Bott kindly, "I can't play with you to-day. I've got other things to do. Anyway, I don't approve of games like that. They're cruel."

"It's not a game," said William. "It's true. He's bein' torchered."

"I don't object to children having their little fancies and imaginings," went on Mrs. Bott, "but you ought to try and think of something pretty, William. Can't you imagine fairies and pretty fairy adventures with flowers and elves and suchlike, instead of things like torturers?"

"I tell you it's Mr. Bott," shouted William excitedly. "Won't you *listen*? It's Mr. Bott who's bein' torchered."

"Now, William, don't talk nonsense," said Mrs. Bott sharply. "You ought to know at your age how wrong it is to tell stories. I *know* that Mr. Bott's in Scotland,

"WHATEVER MISCHIEF HAVE YOU BEEN IN NOW, WILLIAM?"
SAID MRS. BOTT.

because I had a picture post card from him this
morning."

"I don't care. He *is* bein' torchered," persisted
William. "I've seen him to-day through a window. In a
house jus' the other side of Marleigh. He was lyin' on a

table, an' a big man was pullin' his arms an' legs out of their sockets."

Mrs. Bott looked at him. There was no doubting his sincerity. Beneath its coating of garden soil his face fairly radiated earnestness. She blinked at him helplessly. Her expression registered a mixture of incredulity and apprehension.

"You—you've made a mistake, William," she said faintly. "It—it can't be Mr. Bott."

"I tell you it *is*," said William vehemently. "I know him, an' I've *seen* him bein' torchered. On a table an' his arms an' legs bein' pulled out. I tell you I know. They kidnapped him on his way to Scotland."

Mrs. Bott began to wring her plump hands.

"Oh dear," she said, "oh dear, oh dear. . . . It can't be true off the pictures. Not a thing like this. I can't believe it. William," suddenly becoming stern, "it's very wrong indeed of you to try to frighten me by ridiculous tales like this. Tales that couldn't possibly be true. I'm not at all sure that I won't write and complain to your father about you. Go home at once and wash your face and brush your hair and tidy yourself up. I never saw such a sight as you look."

"Well, I got like this tryin' to rescue him," pleaded William passionately. "Won't you come an' *see*, anyway?"

There was something very impressive in William's tone and expression. Mrs. Bott raised her hand to her head.

"It's the sort of thing one dreams of after lobster mayonnaise," she said faintly. "I can't believe it, William. It's impossible. I mean—well, if a thing's impossible, it's impossible, isn't it? I'll show you the picture post card I had from him this morning. It's got Highland cattle on. Ever so pretty. He'd never have sent it if he'd been kidnapped."

"Well, won't you jus' come an' *see*?" said William again.

Mrs. Bott put her hand on the bell.

"Now if I find you've been making all this up, William," she said, "I'll go *straight* to your father."

In a few minutes Mrs. Bott and William were speeding along the road in Mrs. Bott's Rolls Royce. They looked an odd couple. William's collar and tie were still at unconventional angles. His face was still adorned with garden soil, his dishevelled hair (despite the butler's attention) with laurel leaves. Mrs. Bott, who was now in a highly emotional state, had put on her large be-feathered hat anyhow. Her face was flushed, her eyes protruded.

"We'd better stop here," said William, when the car had reached the beginning of the bottle-crowned wall. "If you drive right up, it'll put them on their guard an' they'll hide him. . . ."

Mrs. Bott showed every symptom of going into hysterics, then, realising that there was no suitable audience, mastered herself.

"Now, William," she said, "if I find he's not here, I'll never forgive you. No, I don't mean that, but—I mean I'll never forgive you for this awful half-hour you've given me. I'll go straight and tell your father."

"He's here all right," said William, stepping out of the car. "You come with me."

Mrs. Bott followed him to the door in the wall. Cautiously he opened it. The kitchen garden was empty. He led the way to the hedge, then across the lawn to the house.

"Now we'll look in the windows," he whispered, "an' I bet we'll soon see him bein' torchered."

Keeping well within the shelter of the bushes, they

looked at the elegantly appointed drawing-room and the elegantly appointed dining-room, but saw no signs of Mr. Bott. In the next room, however, a man lay upon the table, and the man in the white coat stood by him, pulling his arms and legs in the same ungentle fashion as William had seen him pulling Mr. Bott's.

"There," he said, "didn't I tell you?"

"But that's not him," said Mrs. Bott, again wavering upon the verge of hysterics, "that's not my Botty."

"No, but it *shows*, doesn't it?" said William.

He led her to the next window, a long French window, and there upon a sort of slab they saw—unmistakably—Mr. Bott, practically naked, being pummelled unmercifully by an enormous giant of a man. His face was twisted into agonised contortions. Faint groans reached the watching pair. Immediately a tornado burst into the room. Mrs. Bott flung herself through the French window and upon the pummelling giant, beating at him with her fists and screaming: "You leave my Botty alone, you great big bully, you!"

Pandemonium followed, and William flung himself zestfully into the *mêlée*, hitting out right and left.

The man in the white coat appeared, and Mrs. Bott at once left the giant and attacked him. Her strength, however, had spent itself upon the giant, and her attack upon the white-coated man was lacking in verve. Comparative order gradually ensued. Mr. Bott lay on the floor, propped up against a wall; Mrs. Bott, her hair falling about her face, knelt beside him, panting.

"Oh, Botty," sobbed Mrs. Bott, "have they killed you?"

"Nearly," said Mr. Bott with a moan.

"Madam—" began the man in the white coat, but Mrs. Bott cut him short angrily.

"Don't you dare speak to me. I've got the house

surrounded by aeroplanes and armoured cars, so you might as well surrender." Then, turning to her husband: "Oh, Botty, how did you come to this awful place? Did they kidnap you on the way to Scotland?"

"No," said Mr. Bott faintly, "I came—I came for treatment."

"For what?" said his wife.

"For treatment, my dear. You know how you've often said you'd like me to get my weight down. Well, I heard they did it for you here and I wanted it to be a little surprise. I—well, my dear, I meant it to be a little birthday present for you."

"But what *is* this place?" said Mrs. Bott hysterically.

The giant had gone, and the man in the white coat stood leaning against the mantelpiece and watching them with an expression of aloof disdain. William was eagerly examining the appointments of the room. He thought that it would be useful to him in his career at Scotland Yard to know exactly what a torturer's den looked like. He had just decided that a reading stand that happened to be standing in a corner was a particularly ingenious thumb-screw.

"It's a Nature Cure place," said Mr. Bott. "They do osty-something-or-other and massage and diet. Oh, my dear"—he groaned again—"the diet!"

"What diet, dear?" said Mrs. Bott solicitously.

"Starvation," groaned Mr. Bott. "They call it diet, but it's starvation. *Starvation*, pure and simple. For three days—for three—whole—days I had nothing but orange juice."

"Botty!" screamed Mrs. Bott, in sympathetic anguish. "Oh, *Botty*!"

"Nothing but orange juice," repeated Mr. Bott, dwelling with morbid relish on his harrowing experiences; "not a crumb of solid food—not one single crumb; nothing but orange juice for three—whole—days. I've never felt so empty in my life. I simply can't describe the feeling, my love. A sort of hollow ache."

"Oh, Botty!" sobbed his sorrowing wife.

"Then after those three days I began to have solid food," went on the sufferer, "but—oh, my dear, you'd hardly call it food. Raisins for breakfast! Just *raisins*! You know, my dear, the things they put in cakes. Fancy making a *meal* of them. A man my size. *Raisins*! And they won't even let me eat as many as I like of them. And raw carrots for dinner. Just imagine! Raw carrots! Then all this banging and pulling about. I can't *tell* you what I've been through."

"Oh, Botty, why didn't you let me *know*?"

"I meant it as a surprise for you, love. I wanted it to be a birthday present—me coming home with my figure back. They told me that they could take off a stone a fortnight at these places. So I only pretended to go to Scotland, and I sent some post cards to James there to send to you, so that you'd think I'd gone."

"Oh, Botty, how you must have *suffered*."

"Well, I *have* suffered, love. I won't deny it . . . but I was doing it for your sake. I thought it would be such a nice surprise for you."

Mrs. Bott clung to him in tempestuous affection.

"Oh, Botty! I don't want you any different. I don't reelly. I'll never bother you any more to get your weight down. Oh, I can't bear to think what you've been through."

She turned with a suddenly assumed hauteur to the man in the white coat, who still leant nonchalantly against the mantelpiece.

"You must release my husband at once," she said, "or I'll summon the police."

The man in the white coat smiled.

"You seem to have an entirely mistaken conception of the situation, madam," he said. "Your husband applied for admission to this establishment and has been at liberty to depart from it every moment since he entered it. Personally, I shall view his departure with equanimity. I have realised for some time that he is not likely to reflect any credit upon it. He never goes out for

"TO THINK THAT IF IT HADN'T BEEN FOR THIS DEAR BOY I SHOULDN'T HAVE KNOWN ANYTHING ABOUT IT," SAID MRS. BOTT.

his prescribed walk without stopping at every other shop to guzzle cream buns—a proceeding, I need hardly say, that is strictly forbidden by our rules."

"It's a lie," said Mr. Bott, but he avoided the eyes of the man in the white coat as he said it, and his expression spoke unmistakably of guilt.

"Well, if he did, I'm glad," said Mrs. Bott pugnaciously. "It's probably the only thing that's kept him alive. He'd be dead by now if he hadn't done. . . ."

She looked round and suddenly realised William's

THE MAN IN THE WHITE COAT SCOWLED AT WILLIAM.

presence. He was engaged in taking to pieces a clock that
he suspected of being an elaborately contrived instrument of torture. A cut he had received from one of the
smaller wheels had almost justified his suspicions. The
reading stand, reduced to its component parts, lay in the
middle of the floor.

"Your young friend's activities," said the man in the
white coat pleasantly, "will be added to the bill."

Mrs. Bott turned to William with outstretched arms.

"To think that if it hadn't been for this dear boy I
shouldn't have known anything about it. I shall always
believe that he saved your life, Botty." She pressed
William's reluctant head against her large, soft, perfumed bosom. "I shall never forget what I owe to you,
dear boy. Never, never, never."

*　　*　　*

William walked slowly homeward. He had decided
not to run away to sea. He had decided not even to go to
Scotland Yard. He had come to the conclusion that as
thrilling adventures can be found on one's own door-
step as anywhere. In one evening he had laid bare a
dastardly plot to starve and torture a respectable
inhabitant of his native village, and by his quickness and
resource had assured the rescue of that citizen. He
remembered Mrs. Bott's words—"I shall never forget
what I owe to you, dear boy. Never, never, never." The
utmost possible must be made of the promise contained
in her words. William's brain was already at work
devising how much could be made of it, and how long
her mood of gratitude could be counted on to last.
Certainly this was no moment to be running away from
home. There was a smile of happy anticipation on his lips
as he walked along. . . .

Chapter 3

Mistakes Will Happen

Relations between Robert and William were very strained, and William was rather troubled by the fact. At an ordinary time it would not have troubled him—it was indeed a natural and usual state of affairs—but it was not an ordinary time. It was a momentous and important time. It was the week before William's birthday, and William knew that Robert, if annoyed, was quite capable of letting the day pass without any tangible tribute to it. It had happened before, and William knew that, unless Robert's wrath were assuaged, it would happen again. There was perhaps reason for Robert's wrath. Even William admitted that. . . .

Robert had been acting in a dramatic entertainment organised by the local football club. The play was a thriller of a highly complicated sort, freely interspersed with screams and pistol shots and mysterious failures of the electric lights. Every character in it who tried to telephone found the cord cut, and whenever the electric lights did function, shadows of strange, bat-like figures were seen passing to and fro outside the window—a phenomenon that remained unexplained throughout the play.

The culminating moment of horror, however, was when a curtain covering a recess was withdrawn and Robert was discovered hanging head downwards on a chair, his shirt front drenched in red ink. The moment was led up to very dramatically. . . . The whole of the

cast gathered round the curtain, obviously in a state of
extreme apprehension. One and then another
approached the curtain as if to withdraw it, then shrank
back, registering terror by both gesture and expression.
Finally one brave spirit pulled the curtain and to the
accompaniment of screams and groans discovered
Robert upside-down, bathed in red ink. The heroine and
her sister fainted—a sofa and easy chair being put on the
stage specially to receive them—and then the curtain
dropped and brought Act II to an end. Robert did not
appear in this act till its culminating moment, and he
naturally did not wish to spend the half-hour or so before
the culminating moment upside-down, bathed in ink, or
even sitting cramped in a tiny chair between the drawn
curtain and a French window that was apt to collapse at a
touch. Moreover, he was in charge of the refreshments,
and this half-hour gave him a chance to superintend the
preparation of the coffee and sandwiches that were
served to the audience after the play. He therefore
engaged William (at a fee of a penny each time) to sit on
the chair behind the curtain till the moment of the
dénouement approached, and then come and warn him
in time for him to take his place upside-down with his
head touching the floor.

William's cue for fetching Robert was "My God,
what's behind that curtain?" said in a shrill falsetto
(meant to express extreme terror) by Dorita Merton, a
girl with very golden hair and very blue eyes, who was
Robert's latest flame.

This went off very well at the rehearsals and at the first
performance. William listened intently for his cue and
fetched Robert at the right moment, in good time to be
discovered upside-down, drenched in red ink, to the
accompaniment of the shrieks and groans of the whole
cast.

It was on the second and last performance that the fiasco occurred. The novelty had worn off the situation, and William was growing rather tired of it. Moreover, he was haunted by a terrible suspicion that if he had held out Robert might have increased his fee to twopence.

He had now heard the play six times and he was beginning to think that he could have written a much better one himself. Still—he fully intended to carry out his bargain and on the second night he settled himself comfortably in the arm-chair behind the curtain with an orange and a volume of the latest adventures of Sexton Blake.

William afterwards affirmed that Dorita Merton never said "My God, what's behind that curtain?" He said that if she had said it he couldn't possibly have missed it. Some members of the cast agreed that Dorita had omitted it, but others said that she had not. They said that they remembered hearing her say it quite distinctly. And anyway, they added, that was no excuse for William, because he ought to have been following the play carefully behind his curtain and have known that it was time to fetch Robert whether Dorita said "My God, what's behind that curtain?" or not.

Whatever the rights and wrongs of the case, the fact remains that when the curtain was withdrawn, in the carefully worked up atmosphere of horror and mystery, all that could be seen was a small boy in a tweed suit, leaning back comfortably in an arm-chair, eating an orange with considerable gusto and reading a novelette. This sight seemed hardly sufficient to account for the screams and shrieks of terror with which the actors—continuing to play their parts with true British doggedness—greeted it.

Robert, of course, was furious. The second night audience was much more important than the first night audience. All the officials of the football club were there. All Dorita's relations and his own were there. Everybody who was anybody was there, and William, said Robert, had disgraced him—Robert—for ever. Never again, he said, would he hold up his head. His whole life was ruined. Nothing awaited him but a dishonoured old age brought upon him prematurely by William. Nobody, said Robert, would ever talk about anything else for the rest of his life. They'd all tell other people and the other people would tell other people till the news had spread all over England, till he couldn't go anywhere in the whole world where people weren't laughing at him. It was no use doing anything at all with his life now. It was ruined. Absolutely ruined. Even if he invented anything or was made Prime Minister people would only laugh at him now after this.

William bore this tirade with comparative meekness, only persisting to affirm that Dorita had not said "My God, what's behind that curtain?"

It was Dorita, of course, who gave the situation its peculiar bitterness. For Dorita, too, considered herself disgraced for ever by William's unfortunate mistake and, most unfairly, blamed Robert for it.

"I'd invited every friend I'd got in the world to it," she lamented; "and I'd invited a friend of my uncle's who knows a man who knows Cochran's cousin, and I was sure it would lead to something, because everyone says I have a talent for acting and I know I have myself, and it's just a question of people like Cochran hearing about you, and now my uncle's friend just goes into roars of laughter whenever anyone mentions the wretched play, and, if Cochran does hear about it, it will be just as a joke, and it's perhaps the only chance I'll ever have all my life of getting famous and all spoilt through you."

"IT'S THE ONLY CHANCE I'LL EVER HAVE OF GETTING FAMOUS,"
SAID DORITA, "AND IT'S SPOILT THROUGH YOU."

"Through me?" said Robert indignantly. "You mean
through William. And you couldn't possibly feel worse
about it than I do. . . ."

"Oh, couldn't I?" said Dorita. "How do you know I
couldn't, considering you don't know what I feel. I can't
think why you ever let him sit there like that. Anyone
with any real feeling for acting would have wanted to *act*
the part, not sneak out of it half the time like you did."

"Do you mean I ought to have hung down from a

chair like that with my head on the floor for half an
hour?" said Robert.

"Why not?" said Dorita. "Any *real* actor would
have."

"I'd be dead if I'd done that," said Robert.

Dorita gave a sniff, implying that that would not have
been any great calamity.

But gradually another subject replaced the play fiasco
in Dorita's mind. It was a series of Shakespearian
tableaux that was being given by the school which both
William and her own small brother attended.

"They're doing a scene from King John," she said,
"and I do hope they choose Georgie to be Arthur. He's
such a dear little boy. Just the type for it, you know. *Ever*
so sweet. There's some talk of them choosing his cousin,
who's in the same form and who's a perfectly hateful
little boy. We shall all be most *terribly* upset if they
choose his cousin. I don't really mind them not choosing
either, but if they choose Georgie's cousin instead of
Georgie, I shall simply die. We'll all simply die."

Robert, relieved that she had ceased to harp upon the
unfortunate episode of the play, expressed interest and
sympathy.

"I'm sure they'll choose your brother," he said.

"You'll do what you can about it, anyway, won't
you," she pleaded, "because Georgie's such a *sweet*
little boy?"

"Er—yes," he said, "I'll certainly do what I can. But
I'm afraid I can't do much. You see, I'm not connected
with the school in any way."

"But your brother goes there," she said.

"Y-yes," he admitted. "He does go there, but—he
hasn't actually got much influence there."

"Yes, but he *might* be able to do something, mightn't
he?"

Robert admitted very doubtfully that perhaps he might. . . .

The next day, however, it turned out that another boy, by name Herbert Frances, had been chosen to play Arthur. Dorita, whose entire interest was now concentrated upon the affair, rang up Robert to tell him about him.

"Of course, I feel dreadful in a *way*," she said earnestly, "because this boy they've chosen isn't *half* as sweet as Georgie, but—well, of course, I'd feel *much* worse if they'd chosen his cousin, because my aunt's very silly and seems to think that he's cleverer than Georgie, and really Georgie's heaps the cleverest of the two."

Robert was beginning to tire of the subject of Georgie, but he was grateful to it for ousting the subject of the play, and he was as much enthralled as ever by the very golden hair and very blue eyes of Dorita.

Now that the question of Georgie appeared to be settled, Robert again began to try to lead the interest of the beloved into more congenial regions—regions of dances and motor runs and pictures and *tête-à-tête* in general. Dorita was showing every sign of being willing to have her interest led into these regions and all was merry as a marriage bell when suddenly the Georgie question popped up again.

When Robert called for the beloved one afternoon he found her pale and distraught.

"That boy who was going to be Arthur has got a dreadful cold," she said, "and if it doesn't get well before the day he can't possibly be in it. And they say that it's between Georgie and his cousin again. Oh *dear*, it's so trying. I thought it was all settled. I tell you if they choose Georgie's cousin I shall *die. Literally* die. Georgie's so sweet and his cousin's the most *hateful* little wretch."

Robert tried again to whip up interest in the Georgie-Arthur question.

"Oh, they'll choose Georgie," he said. "I'm sure they'll choose Georgie."

"But *will* they?" said Dorita gloomily. "People are so *unfair*, you know. And Georgie *is* so sweet. He honestly is. We *all* think so."

In vain Robert tried to lead her attention back to dances and motor rides and cinemas and *tête-à-tête* in general. It refused to leave Georgie. The day of the entertainment drew nearer, and Herbert's cold—despite the attentions of his whole family, who poured out upon him in an unending stream every remedy for a cold that was suggested to them by a large and interested circle of friends—grew no better. His nose and eyes continued to be a fiery red, he continued to sneeze incessantly and to assure everyone at frequent intervals, but more and more indistinctly each time, that he was "a liddle better dow, thag you."

Dorita's excitement rose to fever pitch.

"I know that boy's not going to be fit to do Arthur," she assured Robert; "and if they don't choose Georgie I don't know what I shall do. I don't talk much about it," she added, "because I'm one of those people who feel things very deeply, but don't say much. I'm very reserved, you know. . . . Of course, it's the thought of Georgie's cousin that really worries me. I may not have said much about it"—Robert gasped, then quickly changed his gasp to a cough—"but it's in my mind all the time and—" She looked at him reflectively. "Do you know, if this boy's cold *is* too bad for him to be Arthur on the day and they choose Georgie's cousin instead of Georgie, I shall really begin to feel that you've brought me bad luck, because nothing's really gone right with me since that wretched play."

This remark made Robert, on his side, deeply thoughtful. He gathered from it that if Georgie were not chosen as Arthur his chances of continuing to be Dorita's favoured escort were pretty slender.

That evening he cautiously sounded William. William, however, was not responsive. He professed an utter indifference to the doings of the preparatory department of his school. He did not know Herbert Frances, he did not know Georgie, he did not know Georgie's cousin. He did not, moreover, want to know them. He knew nothing about the tableaux, and he had no intention of demeaning himself so far as to attend the performance. His attitude made Robert still more thoughtful. On the evening before the performance he approached William casually and said:

"Oh, by the way, William, it's your birthday next week, isn't it?"

William agreed that it was. There was a faint gleam of hope in his eye.

"What would you like for a present?" continued Robert. William considered this question in silence for a moment. He could hardly believe that Robert really intended to give him a present after the affair of the play, and he was aware that to mention something too expensive would prejudice his chances of getting anything at all.

"Well," he said modestly, "I'd like any little thing. . . . I've had my mouth organ took off me in school by old Stinks and he won't give it me back."

"Of course," said Robert loftily, "you must expect that sort of thing if you make a nuisance of yourself . . . but I may possibly get you another. I won't say I will. It all depends on how you behave between now and your birthday. . . . By the way, with regard to those theatricals at your school, I hear that there's every possibility that Herbert Whoever-he-is won't be able to take the part of Arthur and that it will lie between Georgie Merton and his cousin. Personally, of course, I hope that Georgie Merton will have the part, because I believe that he'd be much more suitable."

Then Robert walked away, leaving William sunk in thought. William, of course, fully understood the trend of Robert's remarks. If he could somehow or other bring it about that Georgie Merton and not his cousin should take the place of Herbert in the preparatory department's tableaux, then Robert would give him a mouth organ as a reward.

That afternoon after school he walked through the playground of the preparatory department, in order to take a brief survey of its inhabitants and discover if possible which of them was Georgie Merton. He walked through in ostentatious aloofness, examining the sky above him or the ground beneath him, scorning to appear to be taking any interest in the doings of the inferior mortals around him. But, despite his pretended absorption, he sent quick glances of enquiry to right and left as he passed on his way. Suddenly he came upon two small boys fighting. The smaller one was fighting gamely and in accordance with the rules of fair play. The other one was kicking and punching wildly and yet was getting the worst of it. William took to the smaller one at once. He had a merry, impudent, freckled face and a twinkle in his eyes. William felt instinctively that, despite his youth, he was the right sort of person to be wrecked on a desert island with. That was William's unvarying criterion of character. If a new acquaintance did not strike William as the right sort of person to be wrecked on a desert island with, then William had no further use for him, whatever his other talents and accomplishments.

The other boy had a mop of auburn curls and long, effeminate eyelashes. He was fat and flabby and pale, and looked furtive and bad-tempered. Old ladies would probably have raved over his curls and long lashes, thought William, in a lightning summing up of his character, but on a desert island he would be worse than useless.

"Here!" said William to him sternly, "can't you fight properly without kicking?"

He looked at William open-mouthed, then turned and fled with a howl of terror. The other boy gave William a friendly grin.

"What's you name?" said William.

"George Merton," said the boy.

"And who's the other boy?"

"My cousin," said George. "He and I hate each other. We fight every day. He kicks like that because he can't beat me unless he does."

"I thought you were fighting jolly well," said William approvingly, and passed on his way.

He felt much cheered and encouraged. George Merton was a boy after his own heart. It would be a welcome task to assure that he and not the obnoxious cousin should play Arthur. William, of course, had no idea how to set about this. He decided that the only thing to do at present was to hover near the preparatory department to catch such news as leaked out from it.

The news that leaked out that night was that Herbert's mother was certain that he would be quite well enough to play Arthur by to-morrow. She had bought a new medicine that was guaranteed to cure a cold in one night and she was giving Herbert a double dose to make quite sure.

William, going away with this news, came upon George Merton looking for caterpillars in the hedge.

They conversed for a few minutes and discovered many tastes and ideals in common. George, too, disliked civilisation and had decided to discover and reign over a hitherto undiscovered island when he was grown up.

"An' I'm not goin' to have people washin' and brushin' their hair an' bein' polite all day in *my* country," he said firmly; "there's goin' to be a law against it."

"That's a jolly good idea," agreed William, and added: "Do you want to be Arthur of whatever he is in this ole tableau if Herbert can't be it?"

George grinned.

"I wouldn't for myself," he said, "only if I'm not it my cousin will be, an' he'll crow over me for all he's worth. They're always goin' on at me, sayin' why don't I keep myself clean an' tidy like what he does, so it'll be jolly well snooks for them if they choose me for the ole tableau an' not him. But anyway Herbert's mother says that he'll be well enough."

"I hope he won't," said William, who was now beginning to feel that that would be too tame an ending to the affair.

The next morning, however, he heard that Herbert's mother had written to say that she was keeping Herbert in bed for the morning and giving him another double dose of the new cure, and that she was quite sure he would be well enough to take the part of Arthur in the afternoon. Still—William liked to be prepared for anything and the evening before he had made a thorough investigation of the precincts of the preparatory department and had laid certain nebulous plans that would depend entirely on circumstances.

The whole school was given a holiday on the afternoon of the performance, and William at once repaired to the preparatory department to see how affairs were going on. All was confusion and pandemonium. Herbert's mother had rung up to say that the new cold cure had upset Herbert's stomach so much that she was afraid that he couldn't possibly come. He'd been sick all morning and was in the process of being sick again. She added that both she and Herbert were bitterly disappointed and that she hoped they would return the money she had paid for her ticket. . . .

A master came out into the playground holding a velvet doublet in his hand. His face wore a desperate and harassed expression. He looked round the seething mass of small boys . . . then his eye fell on William and he brightened. William's purposeful air gave him for the moment a misleading appearance of earnestness and virtue.

"Oh, I say, you!" he called. "Will you fetch me— well, I don't suppose you know any of their names, do you?—but you can't mistake this kid. He's the only kid in the place with red curls. Red curls. Find a kid with red curls for me and tell him to come and get into Arthur's togs at once as the other brat's laid up. I don't see him in the playground, but he may be in the shrubbery. Red curls. You can't mistake him."

William hastened into the shrubbery and there he found the two cousins engaging in their daily fight. The owner of the red curls had just landed a masterly kick in his opponent's stomach. William laid a hand on the red curls and dragged their owner unceremoniously away.

"You're wanted," he said tersely.

"Who wants me?" said the youth, wriggling against William's relentless grip.

"They want you to be Arthur. Come on. I'll show you the way to the dressing-room."

"Ha, ha!" jeered the youth triumphantly. "An' that ole Georgie said they'd choose him. I told him they'd

never choose *his* ugly mug and I was right, wasn't
I?"

"Come on and don't talk so much," said William
shortly, drawing the red head firmly towards a coal-shed
that stood in the farthest corner of the shrubbery.

"This isn't the way to the dressing-room," protested
the youth.

"Yes it is," said William, "They've changed it to
here." He opened the door. "Here it is."

"That's a coal-shed," objected his victim.

But he had entered it in order to make sure that it
really was a coal-shed, and in that second William
slammed the door and thrust the latch home. Angry
shouts arose at once from within, but they were drowned
by the pandemonium from the playground.

William returned to the other end of the shrubbery
and found the other small boy engaged in his search for
caterpillars.

"I say," he greeted William, "I believe this is an
elephant hawk. Is it an elephant hawk? Look at it."

"You've got to come with me," said William,
"you're wanted."

He drew him back to the playground and left him in
the middle of it, saying: "Stay here."

Then he approached the door where the master still
stood gazing round despairingly, dangling the velvet
doublet.

"I can't find anyone with red curls," said William
unblushingly. "That boy was in the shrubbery"—pointing to Georgie who still stood where William had left
him—"but he's not the one, is he?"

The master looked at him and brightened.

"He'll do," he said. "He was in the running. We
tossed up which to have and it came to the other, but this
one will do just as well. Tell him to come to me at once."

William delivered his message, and George, first handing his possible elephant hawk into William's care, went to the door and was hustled out of sight by the master.

William waited outside the main entrance. Pandemonium ceased in the playground and the preparatory department fled into the hall to take their seats. The first members of the audience began to arrive. Robert and Dorita arrived together. William winked and nodded to Robert in order to inform him that all was well. He must make it quite clear to Robert afterwards that he had to run tremendous risks and exercise superhuman cunning in order to bring about this happy consummation. A mouth organ, after all, was very inadequate remuneration. He'd tell Robert that he wanted a camera instead. A *good* camera. Or perhaps it would be best to put the whole thing upon a cash basis. Ten shillings surely wouldn't be too much to ask for a thing like this. Ten shillings at least. . . .

The doors were shut and the performance was beginning. William, who had never intended to pay an entrance fee, hoisted himself up with some difficulty to one of the windows that gave him a partial view of the stage. The tableaux succeeded each other to the accompaniment of hysterical applause from the actors' aunts and sisters and mothers and nurses, who formed the audience.

Then came the tableau from King John with George in a black velvet suit and lace collar. William, craning his neck so as to see Dorita and Robert, threw them a proud and self-congratulatory glance. But Dorita appeared to have been suddenly taken ill. Her eyes bulged, her face went red. She rose and, with a wild glance around, plunged out of the building, followed by the bewildered Robert. She was probably overcome by sheer joy, thought William, dropping from his perch. He must show her the rest of his efforts on his behalf. She must be made to realise what masterly strategy he had displayed. She, too, might feel impelled to place the matter on a cash basis. Ten shillings from Robert and ten shillings from her. . . . It sounded too good to be true, but such things had been known to happen. William himself had once met an actual living boy who had been given a pound by a complete stranger for finding her lost ring. And, even if they couldn't rise to it, he'd still have the mouth organ. . . . He played on an imaginary mouth organ as he waited for them.

They were coming out of the building now.

"I shall never forgive you," Dorita was saying hysterically. "You told me that Georgie had got the part—you *told* me so. . . ."

"Yes, but—but—" began the bewildered Robert.

William had hastened down to the coal-shed. She'd be jolly grateful to him when she saw what he'd done for her. He unlatched the door and the red-haired child came out, howling angrily. But he was red-haired no longer. His attempts to escape from his prison had covered him with coal-dust from head to foot. He was a terrible and sinister object—black and howling. He fled from his prison round the side of the school and straight into Dorita's arms. She screamed wildly.

"Georgie! Oh, *Georgie*! What have they *done* to you?"

"That's not Georgie," explained William patiently, "Georgie's in there actin'. It was me that got him in. An' I got his cousin shut in the coal-shed so's they'd be sure to choose your brother. . . ."

"My brother!" shrieked Dorita, hugging the black-crusted form to her bosom. "*This* is my brother."

"That boy shut me in the coal-shed," howled the

child, pointing to William. "Why doesn't somebody *do* something to him for shutting me in the coal-shed?"

"B-b-but the other one said he was George Merton," stammered William.

"They're *both* called George Merton," screamed Dorita. "You *must* have known they were both called George Merton."

William realised suddenly that he had never even asked the name of the red-headed one. He had been simply George Merton's cousin.

He realised, too, that the situation was past hope and looked round desperately for escape.

"Why doesn't someone *do* something to that boy for shutting me in the coal-shed?" howled the black one again vociferously.

But he was a little less black than he had been before, as he had rubbed a good deal of his coal off on to his sister's pale fawn costume, which she was wearing to-day for the first time. She noticed this suddenly and hurled Georgie from her with horror and disgust.

"Get away," she sobbed in fury, "you hateful, dirty little boy!"

She tore open her bag and glanced at her reflection in her mirror. Her worst suspicions were confirmed. The side of her face that she had rested in sisterly emotion upon Georgie's curls was adorned by a bold smudge of black. Her once white gloves were black. A small piece of coal adhered to her golden hair.

"*Oh!*" she screamed, then with a stamp of her foot, "I shall never speak to any of you again. Never, never, *never*!" Livid with fury beneath her coal-dust, she swung round upon Robert.

"As for you—"

Robert at bay swung round upon William.

"As for *you*—!"

"MY BROTHER!" SHRIEKED DORITA. "THIS IS MY BROTHER."

"B-B-BUT THE OTHER ONE SAID HE WAS GEORGE MERTON,"
STAMMERED WILLIAM.

But William was not there. He was already nearly a quarter of a mile off.

He threw an imaginary mouth organ away from him as he ran.

Chapter 4

William and Cleopatra

William was feeling slightly depressed. He had had a run of bad luck that had culminated in his breaking Miss Hathaway's garden frame by falling into it from the high wall that ran round her garden. High walls always had a fascination for William, especially if they were narrow as well as high. He liked to see how far and how quickly he could walk along them. A tree grew temptingly near this particular wall, and William had climbed the tree, hoisted himself upon the wall and, balancing with outstretched arms, had begun to walk along it. The top had been level, and William had progressed at a pace of which he had been very proud till, yielding to over-confidence, he had attempted to run and had descended heavily into Miss Hathaway's garden frame. Had it not happened that Miss Hathaway was in her greenhouse at the time William might have escaped unnoticed, but as it was, he rose from the bed of the frame to confront an enraged Miss Hathaway, who pointed a watering-can at him accusingly and said:

"Now I've caught you, William Brown. And it's not the first time you've damaged my garden either."

William removed a seedling from his mouth and considered the situation thoughtfully. There had been a recent occasion when he had taken a short cut through Miss Hathaway's garden in order to intercept one of his enemies and, tripping up at an inopportune moment, had fallen into the middle of one of Miss Hathaway's flower-beds, crushing several choice plants in his descent. He had hoped that the incident was unobserved but evidently it had not been. There was one redeeming feature of the present situation, and that was that his father was away and so she could not at any rate complain to him. Her next words, however, destroyed his feeling of security on this score.

"I know your father's away," she said, "but he's coming back on Friday and first thing on Saturday morning I'm going to tell him."

Her expression was grim and unrelenting.

"But, listen," pleaded William eagerly, "just listen. . . ."

She raised her hand in a majestic gesture.

"Not another *word*, William," she said, and, turning on her heel, walked with great dignity into the house.

William bound up a cut knee with a grimy handkerchief, removed some more seedlings from his hair and mouth, and set off slowly homewards. His face, beneath its coating of prepared potting soil, was very thoughtful. His birthday was the Sunday after his father's return, and Mr. Brown had promised to give him ten shillings for his birthday present on condition that he had a good report of his conduct during his absence. William knew that, with the well-known and universal meanness of grown-ups, he would be only too ready to take advantage of Miss Hathaway's complaint and refuse to give William any money at all.

There were only two days before his return. Miss Hathaway's expression had been the expression of one not to be moved from her determination by either reasoning or entreaty. During lunch his mother asked him anxiously why he was so quiet. He replied darkly that he'd jolly well got enough to make anyone quiet, and relapsed again into gloomy silence.

After lunch he went upstairs and spent an hour not only removing all traces of his descent into the garden frame but also putting an added lustre upon his appearance that was little short of startling. He scrubbed his knees till they were sore, he cleaned his nails, he washed his face with pumice-stone to be on the safe side, he "borrowed" Robert's hair oil to stick down his hair, he put on his Sunday suit and a clean collar and tie. Thus resplendent and wearing his most innocent and appealing expression, he set off in the direction of Miss Hathaway's house. He felt hopefully that his appearance should go far to remove the unfortunate impression caused by the morning's escapade. He practised his "polite voice" as he walked along the road, apologising profusely to the hedges on either side of him for having broken their garden frame, stopping earnestly to assure a straying cow that he would repair the damage himself with glue so that it would be even better than new. . . . Soaring to yet higher flights of eloquence and invention he informed a hen crossing the road that he had only climbed the wall because he thought that he had heard a cry for help. It was in fact his eagerness to come to her rescue that had made him fall down upon her garden frame. His spirits rose higher as he neared Miss Hathaway's house. He felt that no one—not even Miss Hathaway herself—could resist such an appeal as he was going to make. By the time he had reached her front door he had fully persuaded himself that he had really climbed the wall in reply to a cry of help, and his expression was an impressive blend of injured innocence and wistful appeal.

The housemaid who opened the door seemed—rather to his chagrin—unmoved by his appearance and expression.

"She doesn't want to see you," she said, and shut the door unceremoniously in his face.

William felt disconcerted by this unexpected turn of events.

He was firmly convinced, however, that Miss Hathaway, once she had heard his story, would not only pardon him but feel actually grateful to him (he was becoming more and more certain that he had heard that cry for help). It was simply a question of persuading her to listen to him. He rang the bell again with great vehemence. The housemaid opened the door, also with great vehemence.

"You be off this minute," she said angrily, "or I'll box your ears."

So ready did she look to fulfil her threat that William flung dignity to the winds and fled precipitately down to the garden gate. In the road he stood throwing stones absently over the hedge and brooding disconsolately on the unfairness of life. All this trouble for nothing, making himself *raw* with cleanness and all for nothing. . . . She wouldn't even listen to him . . . all that fuss about an old garden frame that he'd only broken with trying to come to her rescue . . . it was jolly unfair. A larger stone than usual, despatched over the hedge with a force born of bitterness and disappointment, hit Farmer Jenks, who happened to be crossing the field, neatly on the ear. With a cry of pain and rage Farmer Jenks leapt the stile between the field and the road, and, seeing his old enemy, William, started off in pursuit. William led him zestfully into a neighbouring wood and there let him come almost to grips with him several times before adroitly evading his grasp by dodging round a tree. He finally threw him off by following a stream along its narrow bed under the roadway, and returned home much exhilarated but with

"YOU BE OFF THIS MINUTE," SAID THE HOUSEMAID ANGRILY,
"OR I'LL BOX YOUR EARS."

his pristine spruceness sadly dimmed.

Thinking over the affair of the garden frame, he was
now firmly convinced that Miss Hathaway's housemaid
was his enemy and that out of sheer malice she had
not even told Miss Hathaway of his visit. Generally

speaking, William was not popular with the domestic staffs of his neighbours. They classed him with tramps and gypsies, and showed him as scant courtesy. Yes, the more he thought of it the more convinced he became that it was Miss Hathaway's maid who had denied him admittance, not Miss Hathaway herself. "Frightened prob'ly I'd tread on a carpet or touch somethin'," he said bitterly to himself. "They seem to think you can go about same as a ghost not treadin' anywhere or touchin' anythin'."

He indulged his sense of grievance against Miss Hathaway's maid by imagining a scene in which he captured her at the head of his pirate band, and compelled her to spend the months of her imprisonment cleaning up muddy footmarks that he made purposely every morning. "That'd jolly well *teach* her," he said grimly. But this picture, though a pleasing one, did nothing actually to further the situation, and he set himself seriously to consider what must be done. After much cogitation he decided that the next step was to waylay Miss Hathaway in the village. It would be useless to approach the house again, guarded as it was by the hostile maid. He must waylay Miss Hathaway herself and put his case before her. Surely when she knew that he had only climbed the wall in order to rescue her she would see the matter in a different light. . . . He hung about the village shop the next morning and soon saw Miss Hathaway approaching it on her bicycle. Outside the shop she dismounted. William approached her eagerly.

"Please, Miss Hathaway," he began, trying to preserve the exact balance between eagerness and politeness, "when I climbed your wall the other day it was because—"

She raised her hand in a commanding gesture of

dismissal. "Not another *word*, William." And she passed into the shop, without looking at him.

William, feeling considerably less optimistic than he had felt a few moments before but having by no means given up hope, waited till she came out and then accosted her again.

"Please, Miss Hathaway, about me gettin' on your wall yesterday, I thought I heard—"

Again she raised her hand in the commanding gesture of dismissal.

"Not a *word*, William. I shall complain to your father immediately on his return."

"If you'll jus' *listen*, I can explain—"

But he was addressing the empty air. Miss Hathaway was already pedalling her way down the road, every inch of her thin, angular figure expressing grim resolution.

William realised that it is impossible to waylay a person who refuses to be waylaid. He lacked the optical power of the Ancient Mariner. So despondent did he feel that he even accompanied his mother meekly, and without protest, on a visit to an aunt whom he had always disliked. The aunt, after delivering her usual homily on How Much Better Children Behaved when She was Young, gave him an ancient book of engravings to look through as a great treat. He sat at the table, turning over the leaves morosely. "This is what comes of helpin' people," he said to himself bitterly. "I jolly well won't go the next time I hear her cry for help. Pinchin' all my money off me!" The picture darkened so that he almost believed that Miss Hathaway had deliberately lured him into her garden by a feigned cry for help in order to rob him of his money.

He flicked over the pages one by one, glancing contemptuously at each. Giving him a picture book to look at as if he was a kid! Then he stopped at a picture, examining it with sudden interest. It showed a woman standing on a half-unrolled carpet in front of a Roman general.

"What's this about?" he demanded.

The aunt came over to him and, adjusting her pince-nez, inspected the picture.

"That, William," she said, "is Cleopatra. Caesar had refused to grant her an interview. So she sent him a present of a carpet, and when it was unrolled she was in the middle of it and so he had to grant her the interview. Very foolish and unsuitable. Turn on a few pages, dear, and you'll find a nice picture of shepherds tending their flocks on the hills."

But William was gazing with deepening interest at the picture of Cleopatra arising from the carpet. That was a jolly good idea. He imagined Cleopatra at the door of Caesar's house being turned away by an indignant housemaid . . . accosting him as he descended from his bicycle outside the village shop and being unceremoniously brushed aside . . . and then this idea of a carpet. It was a jolly clever idea. . . . He continued to gaze at the picture till it was time to go home. On his way home he broke a long silence by saying suddenly:

"How much do carpets cost, mother?"

"Pounds and pounds, dear," said Mrs. Brown.

"Aren't there any cheaper than that?" he demanded.

"I suppose you can get very common ones for about a pound, but it wouldn't last any time at all, of course."

"I suppose you couldn't get a very, *very* common one for about sixpence?" asked William hopefully.

"Oh, no, dear, of *course* not," said Mrs. Brown.

William abandoned the idea of the carpet. He abandoned it reluctantly, because the mental picture of himself rising to his feet as the carpet was unrolled and confronting an amazed Miss Hathaway, like Cleopatra in the engraving, was a very pleasant one. He would have explained all about the broken garden frame and the cry for help before she recovered from her astonishment, and she would be overcome by gratitude and penitence.

The more he thought about it the more convinced of this he became. It was simply a question of getting her to listen to him. William had great faith in his eloquence. It was a pity that carpets were so dear. . . .

Though he had now given up his plan of actually making his way into Miss Hathaway's presence enveloped in a carpet, still the general idea seemed to him so good that he had not altogether abandoned it. Surely there must be something cheaper than a carpet that would serve the purpose. . . .

He was ruminating the subject as he went along the road that led past the station the next morning. Suddenly he stopped. An enormous brand-new dog kennel stood there. A most magnificent dog kennel. A very palace of a dog kennel. And there was a dog in it—a friendly brown dog who pushed his nose through the bars that closed up the ornate doorway of the structure. William forgot everything else in his interest in the dog. He knelt down on the ground, playing with it and stroking it through the bars. He found a dusty fragment of biscuit in his pocket and offered it. To his immense delight the dog ate it.

"Like to come out for a run down the road?" he said; "I bet you'd like to come out for a run down the road, wouldn't you?"

The brown dog wagged its tail so expectantly that William felt that he had definitely pledged himself to take it for a little run down the road. He examined the fastenings of the barred gate. Yes, there was a latch that slipped back, and then it opened quite easily. There couldn't be any harm in taking the little dog for a run down the road and back, and then shutting him up in the kennel again.

'Come on," he said as he opened it, "come on for a little run then."

The dog leapt out, curvetting round William's feet joyfully. Attached to his collar was a large luggage label.

"Come on," said William again, setting off at a run down the road. The dog ran on in front of him. It was rather a good runner, and William could barely keep up with it. At the bend in the road he stopped breathlessly. "Now come on back," he said.

But the dog apparently did not hear. It went on at full speed down the road.

"Hi!" shouted William. "Hi! Come back!"

The dog paid no attention. It went on running down the road.

"Hi!" shouted William again, desperately. "Hi! Come back! I'll get into a row if you don't."

This appeal failed to move the dog. It went on running down the road without even looking back. It had now disappeared round the next bend. William panted after it, but the bend showed no brown dog to him. It had vanished completely from the landscape. He struggled on to the cross-roads, but none of the four roads that met there revealed any sign of the brown dog. He walked slowly back to the dog kennel and closed the barred gate, hoping thus to postpone detection of the crime as far as possible. While doing this he caught sight suddenly of the label nailed on to the roof of the kennel: "Miss Hathaway, Laurel Cottage."

Immediately an idea struck him with such overwhelming force that for a moment he actually saw stars. A dog kennel was as good as a carpet. He would go to Miss Hathaway's in the dog kennel. Instead of arising from a carpet, he would crawl out of a dog kennel. And then, before she recovered from her paralysis of amazement, he would make her his apology and explanation. The disappearance of the rightful owner of the kennel was, of course, a slightly awkward feature of the situation, but he hoped to persuade her that it had escaped before the kennel had reached the station. He looked up and down the road. No one was in sight. Obviously the kennel had been put there by the porter to wait for the carrier's cart. Cautiously William unlatched the little barred gate. Yes, it was just large enough to allow him to squirm in. He squirmed in. There was a good deal of straw inside, and somehow not quite as much room as he had thought there would be. Still—he could curl up in it fairly comfortably. He found that there was a little wooden door that could be drawn across the aperture as well as the barred gate. Hearing the sounds of the approach of the carrier's cart he hastily drew it. The kennel lurched wildly and he hit his head with great violence against the side.

"Coo!" he heard a man's voice say. "It ain't 'alf 'eavy. What's in it?"

"Porter said it were a kennel and dawg inside," said another voice.

"It ain't no dawg," said the first voice. "More like bricks by the weight of it. Bricks or coal."

"Coal," said the second voice. "Yes, I bet it's coal. A new-fangled coal-shed made in the shape of a dawg's kennel. Coo, the things they make nowadays!"

This explanation seemed to satisfy both of them, and they hoisted William up on to the cart. To William it was as if the kennel had become suddenly inspired with malignant life and were battering his head from all sides. He protected himself from it as well as he could, then cautiously opened the little wooden door in order to admit some air. The cart rattled and jolted along the road and finally stopped outside Miss Hathaway's house.

Miss Hathaway came out, a shawl wrapped round her head, and stood half-way down the garden path.

"I won't come any nearer," she called to the driver, "I've got the most dreadful cold, and I don't want to give it to anyone. That's the dog kennel, isn't it? It's for my sister's birthday present, and I meant to take it to her myself to-day in a cab, but with this awful cold I can't. Now I want you to take it on to my sister's for me—it's at Upper Marleigh—and kindly give her this note with it, will you? The address is on the envelope."

She came near enough to him to hand him the letter at arm's length, keeping her head well turned away.

"I mustn't come near you," she said, "it's a dreadful cold."

She sneezed three times as if to prove her words, then scurried indoors.

The driver glanced at the address, said "Right, 'm'," started up his horse, and set off towards Upper Marleigh.

William was quite unaware of this interlude. The jolting of the cart had so battered his head that finally he had wrapped it round in straw, completely encasing it. This made him deaf and blind to all around him, and during the interview at Miss Hathaway's he was conscious only of a blessed respite from the murderous assaults of the sides of his kennel upon him. He had no idea even that they had passed Miss Hathaway's house and were now on the way to Upper Marleigh. He thought that it was rather a long journey, but he realised that any journey taken under those particular conditions would seem long.

At last the cart came to a standstill, and he felt the

kennel being lifted down—a little more gently this time—and carried along to the accompaniment of exclamations of surprise at its weight. Then it was set down with a bump that nearly dislocated his neck and he was aware of a babel of voices around him. Miss Hathaway's sister, surrounded by a large concourse of friends and relations who had come to celebrate her birthday, was reading her sister's letter aloud:

DEAR ANGELA,

I send herewith my birthday present. I had meant to bring it myself but, alas, I have a most dreadful cold. I am almost prostrate with it. Well, dear Angela, I hope you will like this kennel and its occupant. I think indeed that you will love the occupant, who is the *sweetest* thing. Please give it a kiss on the end of its nose for me. And now, dear, many happy returns of the day and much love,

From,
YOUR LOVING SISTER.

William, whose head was still encircled in straw, had heard none of this. He believed that he had at last reached Miss Hathaway's house and was preparing the speech that he must deliver as soon as he emerged from his hiding-place. He had drawn away some of the straw from his eyes so that he could see, and had opened the little wooden door and was now fumbling with the barred gate.

"Open it," said someone.

A hand came down and firmly withdrew the barred gate.

William began to crawl out.

A sudden silence fell.

They stared aghast at the straw-covered object that

was slowly emerging. Even its face was shrouded in straw. It rose to its feet and, approaching Miss Hathaway's sister, who bore a strong resemblance to Miss Hathaway, began to speak in a hoarse voice:

WILLIAM CRAWLED OUT AND STOOD UP. A SUDDEN SILENCE FELL.

"I came on to your garden wall 'cause I thought I heard a cry for help. That was why I came on to your garden wall. An' that was how I came to break your garden frame 'cause I was hurrying to get to you 'cause of this cry for help. An'—"

He approached nearer, gesticulating vehemently. She gave a wild scream of terror and started to the door, followed by her guests.

"The police!" she screamed. "The police, quickly!"

"WHAT IS IT?" SAID SOMEONE HYSTERICALLY. THEY ALL
STARED AGHAST AT THE STRAW-COVERED OBJECT THAT HAD
SLOWLY EMERGED.

She fled out of the house, still followed by her terrified
guests.

William unwound the straw from his head and looked
about him. He was alone in a room with a large table laid
for tea. Laid for a generous tea. Iced cake, cakes
composed almost wholly of layers of cream, jellies,
trifles, meringues, chocolate biscuits.

William was bruised from head to foot and his mouth
was full of straw, but the sight of this feast made him

realise that his appetite was unimpaired. He was in fact
hungrier than he had ever been in his life before. He
decided just to try the trifle. He would take so little that
the people wouldn't notice when they came back. He
couldn't think why they'd all run off like that. The whole
situation was inexplicable, and he relinquished all
attempts to understand it. Instead he stared in amazement at the empty dish of trifle. Surely he hadn't eaten
all that! There seemed, however, to be no other explanation of its disappearance. He considered it thoughtfully
for a few moments and then took a spoonful of the jelly.
It was the best jelly he had ever tasted. After some
consideration he decided that now the trifle was gone it
would be as well for the jelly to go too. No one ever
provided jelly at a party without trifle. If there was no
trifle, there might as well be no jelly. He finished it up
quickly and thoroughly, and then considered the rest of
the feast. He was still hungry. As he'd probably get into
trouble for eating the jelly and trifle anyway, he might as
well do the thing properly. He proceeded, therefore, to
do the thing properly. The cake, composed chiefly of
layers of cream, was a very king of cakes. William ate
slice after slice of it. As his hunger was appeased so his
sense of mystification increased. Where was everyone?
Why had they all run away like that? Had Miss Hathaway accepted his explanation or hadn't she? A glance
out of the window deepened his mystification still
further. For this was not Miss Hathaway's house at all.
The garden was not Miss Hathaway's garden. The road
outside this house was not the road outside Miss Hathaway's house.

   As if to sustain him against this shock, William went
back to the table and ate six meringues in quick succession. He noticed that both table and floor were
plentifully bestrewn with straw. He picked one or two

pieces up with a vague idea of lessening the sum total of his iniquities, then desisted and went to the window again. All the people were returning. He stood in the shadow of the curtain to watch them. A policeman headed the procession. Someone in the rear carried the brown dog who had evidently been found and brought to Miss Hathaway. Miss Hathaway herself was there, sneezing copiously, her head still wrapped in a shawl. Someone must have fetched her in order to confront her with her strange birthday gift.

The procession slowed down as it neared the door. William could hear excited voices raised shrilly.

"I tell you it was a gorilla. I'm *sure* it was a gorilla."

"But it spoke."

"Gorillas can speak. Didn't you know that? It didn't talk sense. It just said a gabble of words."

"It said something about garden walls and cries for help."

"Yes, but there wasn't any *sense* in it, was there?"

"I think it was a wild man escaped from some show or other. It looked to me just like one of those wild men you see in shows."

"You couldn't see it. It was covered in straw."

"Yes, but I saw its eyes gleaming wildly through the straw."

"Certainly if it was human, it was mad."

William withdrew from the window.

He was still completely in the dark as to what was happening but he was dimly aware that some great ordeal lay before him.

To fortify himself against it, he put a few handfuls of chocolate biscuits into each pocket and very thoughtfully began to eat the last piece of cream-layer cake.

Chapter 5

The Outlaws and the Penknife

Ginger was feeling aggrieved with life in general and his Aunt Amelia in particular.

Ginger's Aunt Amelia had only lately come to live in the neighbourhood. She had taken a cottage, which she shared with a literary friend, and high hopes had sprung to life in Ginger's breast at their arrival. For Aunt Amelia had not seen him since his babyhood. She was not, as were all his other aunts, conversant with his many crimes and shortcomings. She was, in Ginger's eyes, a clean slate, on which he could write a glorious tale of non-existent virtues and reap such a golden harvest as dutiful nephews may expect from high-minded, if rather short-sighted, elderly aunts.

Her first visit passed off very well. Ginger prepared himself for it with a thoroughness that left his mother speechless with surprise and bewilderment, appearing at tea with a face which he had almost flayed by relentless scrubbing, with hair plastered slickly down by a damp hair-brush, and with even his nails partially, at any rate, cleaned. He spoke and behaved with such an extremity of politeness that it was all his mother could do to conceal her anxiety. Like most mothers, she was continually urging Ginger to supreme heights of perfection, but, whenever he seemed to be approaching them, felt only anxiety for his health, and knew no real peace of mind till he had returned to his normal ways of grubbiness, unpunctuality and lawlessness.

She tried, however, to assume the expression of one whose son behaves always like a perfect little gentleman, refraining, by great effort of self-control, from asking him if he felt quite well, and conquering a strong desire to take his temperature. As far as Aunt Amelia was concerned the afternoon was a great success. She was impressed, if somewhat embarrassed, by Ginger's attentiveness. He hovered over her continually, flourishing a cake-stand and waiting patiently for her to finish what was on her plate. He said "Yes, Aunt Amelia" and "No, Aunt Amelia" in a voice of dulcet winsomeness that his own friends would not have recognised. Moreover, he had the good sense to disappear directly tea was over, well aware that a little of a good thing goes a long way and that a character of perfection is a difficult one to sustain for any length of time.

He was rewarded for the strain that he had undergone by a half-crown that Aunt Amelia pressed into his hand as he said good-bye and by overhearing her say as he closed the door: "What a well-behaved boy!"

So far so good, of course. The half-crown was received by the Outlaws (who always shared tips) with acclamation. But it was soon spent, and Ginger realised that if he meant that source of income to continue indefinitely he must get to work again and go very carefully. The other Outlaws suggested that they, too, should be introduced to Aunt Amelia in order to deepen the impression made by Ginger, but he firmly opposed this suggestion.

"No," he said, "it's jolly hard to carry on like what I did when she came to tea. You couldn't do it. I couldn't do it either if any of you were there. No, you'd better leave it to me."

"All right," said William, "but get on with it. We've spent that half-crown, an' it's about time you were gettin' another out of her. I bet I could do it all right. I can make myself look a good deal cleaner than what you can, 'cause I've not got so many freckles—"

"You *have*," put in Ginger indignantly.

"I haven't. We counted once and I've got twenty less. Anyway, I can make myself look cleaner, 'cause I've got some white paint, an' I can paint over the dirty places on my collar, an' my ears don't stick out so much as what yours do, so it doesn't show so much when they aren't clean."

"Oh, don't they?" said Ginger, stung by this insult. "Well, let me tell you they stick out a jolly sight more."

An attempt to settle this question by physical combat left it still undecided, and the Outlaws, tiring of the subject of Ginger's aunt, turned their attention to the more congenial one of a rat hunt in a neighbouring farm.

But Ginger was aware that it was now time that he once more took up the ticklish task of playing the Perfect Boy to Aunt Amelia. As the Outlaws said, her half-crown was now a memory only and another would be welcome. . . .

The next afternoon he spent half an hour on his personal appearance, wrestling long and hard with a species of indelible mud that seemed to have left its permanent mark on his brow and down one cheek. He then changed his collar, inked that portion of one leg that showed through a hole in his navy blue stocking, got a clean handkerchief, but considerably dimmed its glory by dusting his knees with it, rubbed each shoe hard upon the other stocking, leaving thick grey marks, and finally, completely satisfied with his appearance, set off in the direction of Aunt Amelia's cottage. The way was short and easy, but to Ginger it was as steep and arduous as the proverbial path of virtue, presenting at every step temptations to besmirch his comparatively immaculate appearance by burrowing in ditches, exploring tracks through the undergrowth, and climbing trees. He resisted all these temptations, and walked mincingly along, concentrating his attention on practising what he termed his "polite voice"—saying "Yes, Aunt Amelia", "No, Aunt Amelia", and finally, with a shattering smirk, "Oh, *thank* you, Aunt Amelia. How kind of you!" as with outstretched and (despite vigorous applications of pumice-stone) still very grubby palm he received an imaginary half-crown.

He found Aunt Amelia working in her garden, while, seated at an open window overlooking the tiny lawn, the literary friend sat engaged in literary work. Ginger had never met the literary friend, only seen her in the distance like this, intent upon her work, occasionally raising her eyes soulfully to the tree-tops for inspiration. The literary friend wrote stories about an imaginary little boy called Michael—stories that were very much admired by elderly maiden ladies—but disliked children in real life.

"No, dear," she had said to Ginger's aunt, "don't introduce him to me. I find that real children absolutely *kill* my inspiration. There's no—no spiritual *fragrance* about them. I find that *nothing* kills my inspiration as much as a real child. I draw my inspiration from Nature alone."

"But he's a very well-behaved child," Aunt Amelia had said.

"I can't help it, dear," replied the literary friend simply. "I feel absolutely certain that there's no spiritual fragrance about him."

Ginger's aunt had to admit that perhaps there wasn't.

"But he's the politest and best-behaved child I have

ever come across," she repeated.

As Ginger entered the garden, the literary friend slightly shifted her position so that she need not look at him. Certainly, despite his careful grooming, not even his best friend could have said that he suggested spiritual fragrance.

Aunt Amelia greeted him kindly, but abstractedly. It was evident that her whole attention was concentrated upon her gardening operations. With a small knife she was severing shoots from the base of the rose bushes.

"They're briar shoots, dear boy," she explained. "If allowed to grow, they would take all the goodness from the rose bush and finally kill it. It's one of those little things that a gardener can't afford to neglect. And it's a parable—isn't it, dear boy? These little briar shoots are like the little faults that, if we allowed them to grow, would finally take all the goodness from our characters. . . ."

Ginger steeled himself to endure a spate of moralising, sustaining an expression faithfully copied from William and of which William was very proud. It was an expression that was intended to convey radiant virtue and high endeavour, but that actually suggested acute dyspepsia. He consoled himself for the effort involved in keeping up this expression by fixing his thought on the hoped-for half-crown and its many possibilities.

"Such little faults as idleness," said Aunt Amelia.

"An' we'll jolly well get a new ball," thought Ginger, "one of those little ones that we can play with in ole Fuss-pot's history lessons."

"And greed," said Aunt Amelia.

"And some cream buns and liquorice all-sorts," thought Ginger.

"While courtesy and consideration for others," said Aunt Amelia, "are like the healthy rose shoots that will

flourish and grow stronger and stronger if we keep the
briar shoots well cut away."

"An' we'll get some squibs an' throw 'em down at
people after dark," thought Ginger.

"And so, dear boy, we must cut away our briar shoots
and strive ever upwards, and soon we will find our rose
bushes strong and healthy and shining through the
darkness around us, an example to others far and wide."

With this final flourish of mixed metaphors Aunt
Amelia looked at her watch and took up her gardening
basket with an air of finality.

"Did you come for anything special, dear boy?" she
said.

"Yes," said Ginger absently, thinking of the half-
crown, then added hastily: "No, I mean no. I mean"—
intensifying the dyspeptic leer—"I mean I jus' came to
see you."

"Very sweet of you, dear boy," said Aunt Amelia
vaguely, "but I have to go in and write some letters now,
so I'll say good-bye. I can't ask you to come in, because
my friend must have absolute quiet for her work. Good-
bye, dear boy."

With that she went into the cottage, leaving Ginger
gazing at the closed door, the dyspeptic leer frozen upon
his face. Crestfallen, he turned and walked back to the
village, where William and Henry and Douglas were
waiting for him.

"Well?" said William. "How much did she give
you?"

"Nothin'," said Ginger morosely. "I spent hours
gettin' clean an' tidy—my face still aches with washin'—
an' she's not given me a ha'penny."

They looked at him sternly.

Despite his dejection he had on his homeward way
deliberately succumbed to all the temptations, ditch-

"I SPENT HOURS GETTIN' CLEAN AN' TIDY," SAID GINGER, "AN
SHE'S NOT GIVEN ME A HA'PENNY."

burrowing, tree-climbing and undergrowth-exploring,
that he had resisted on his way to the cottage, and the
process had completely obliterated the never-very-strik-
ing effect of cleanliness that he had attained with such
labour.

"Well, of course, if you went lookin' like *that*—" said
William succinctly.

"I didn't go like this," said Ginger indignantly. "I
went lookin' cleaner than you've ever looked in your
life, only I wasn't goin' to bother to keep all that

cleanness on when she wouldn't even give me half a crown for it, so I got it wore off on the way home."

"Well, did you *do* anything for her?" said William.

"No, there wasn't anything to do. . . ."

"That doesn't matter," said William sternly. "You ought to have *done* something for her. They always feel more like givin' you money if you've *done* something for them. You ought to have chopped up wood or weeded a bed or something."

"Yes, like what you did for your aunt," said Ginger indignantly, "an' pulled up all the plants she'd jus' put in an' chopped up some wood she'd jus' bought to do poker work on an' got into a jolly row. Likely she'd have given me half a crown then, isn't it?"

William, faced with these undeniable truths, became evasive.

"Oh, well, I can't stay here all day arguin' with you. Let's go an' do somethin' a bit more interestin'. We don't want her rotten old half-crown, anyway."

So the Outlaws went and did something more interesting, and completely forgot Ginger's aunt and her non-forthcomingness in the matter of half-crowns. All except Ginger. A sense of failure nagged at Ginger's heart, an overmastering desire to return to the fray and prove himself victor. When he could hold out against this desire no longer, he cleaned himself up again secretly, and set off to Aunt Amelia's cottage. He found it deserted, Aunt Amelia evidently having accompanied the literary friend on one of those Nature-communing expeditions that were necessary for the refreshment of her muse. Nothing daunted, Ginger looked about him. Though William himself had certainly had no striking success in his attempts to gain tips by gardening and wood-cutting, there had been sound sense in his advice. Surely Aunt Amelia, confronted on her return by some definite service performed for her in her absence by Ginger, would hardly have the nerve to withhold an honorarium. He looked around the neat little garden, and remembered suddenly the task upon which Aunt Amelia had been engaged on his last visit. He examined the rose trees. Now Ginger was not interested in gardening. He did not go in for fine and subtle distinctions. Briar shoots and shoots of the true rose were all the same to him. So intent had he been on the imaginary expenditure of the hoped-for half crown that he had not listened to a word of the eloquent dissertation that Aunt Amelia had made on his last visit. He remembered the one fact that she had been cutting off shoots from the base of the rose bushes. Therefore, deduced Ginger, shoots ought to be cut off from the base of the rose bushes, and she would be grateful to him for doing it. An inspection of the rose bushes showed them to be in a terrible state of neglect. From the base of each sprang stout and healthy shoots. Ginger's spirits rose at thus finding a useful job ready to hand, a job that, he thought hopefully, should be worth at least half a crown to Aunt Amelia.

It was fortunate that it was his week for the Knife. The Knife was a magnificent affair with four blades, a corkscrew, a file, and a thing for getting stones out of a horse's hoof. William and Ginger shared it, having put together their pocket-money for several weeks in order to buy it. It was their most treasured possession, and they had it for a week each in turn. Though this arrangement led to a certain amount of recrimination, each one zealously examining the instrument after its week's absence and blaming his co-owner for any marks of wear that it might have acquired in the interval, the arrangement on the whole worked out quite satisfactorily. This week it happened to be Ginger's week.

Proudly he took out the treasure, opened the largest blade, and set to work upon the rose shoots.

He worked with commendable industry and thoroughness, and the little heap of rose shoots in the middle of the lawn grew to a fair-sized stack. It was while he was at work upon the last bush that Aunt Amelia returned. She stood for a moment transfixed with horror, gazing at the scene of desolation, then with a cry of rage and anguish flung herself upon the astonished Ginger, snatching the knife from his hand.

"You *wretch*," she screamed, "you've *ruined* my rose trees—*ruined* them! You hateful, *hateful* little wretch!"

She shook Ginger till his teeth chattered, then pushed him from her with a gesture of abhorrence and bent over the heap of rose shoots in an attitude of abandoned despair.

Ginger, who thought that she had suddenly gone mad and was feeling thankful to be escaping with his life, had picked himself up and reached the gate when suddenly he remembered the Knife. Aunt Amelia's frenzy had inspired him with such terror that as far as concerned himself, he would actually have forgone his beloved possession, but there was William to think of. William's week for the Knife began that very evening, and greater even than his terror of Aunt Amelia despoiled of her rose shoots was his terror of William despoiled of his knife.

His collar burst open by the violence of his shaking, his tie under one ear, his hair standing straight on end and his eyes carefully measuring the distance to the open gate, he approached Aunt Amelia, who was still bending over the stack of rose shoots in an attitude suggestive of Rachel mourning for her children.

"Please," said Ginger hoarsely, "can I have my knife back?"

Aunt Amelia swung round on him.

"No, you mayn't," she said hysterically. "*Never*. You shall *never* have your knife back. You wicked, wicked, *wicked* boy!"

Fearing another attack, Ginger took to his heels and ran all the way to the village, without stopping for breath or looking back once.

"YOU SHALL NEVER HAVE YOUR KNIFE BACK," SAID AUNT
AMELIA, "YOU WICKED, WICKED BOY!"

The interview with William was a heated one. Ginger took the line of self-defence. "Well, I was doin' jus' what she was doin'. '*Xactly* what she was doin'. Well, you can't blame me for her suddenly goin' mad, can you? I 'spect she'll be in an asylum to-morrow. She as near killed me as I've ever been. My head as near as possible came right off. You ought to be glad that I've escaped out of the jaws of death 'stead of makin' all this fuss over the knife."

"Well, I'm not," said William. "You could have stayed in the jaws of death for all I care, an' jolly well serve you right. I don't care if your head had come off. It doesn't seem much good on—lettin' her keep a knife like that, we're never likely to have another as good as long as we live."

"I didn't let her keep it. She snatched it off me, ravin' an' carryin' on like a mad woman, though all I'd done was '*xactly* what she was doin' herself when I went there before. I keep tellin' you I can't help people goin' mad. If you know how to stop people goin' mad p'raps you'll kin'ly tell me. Anyway it was all your fault tellin' me to go round an' do somethin' for her. Well, I went round an' did somethin' an' this is what happens."

"Oh, it's all my fault, is it?" said William. "You go an' lose that knife jus' when my week for it's comin' round an' you say it's my fault."

The short, sharp struggle that followed considerably relieved their feelings, and they sat down by the roadside to discuss the question amicably.

"We've gotter get it back," said William firmly. "We can't go on letting her keep a knife like that. I shun't be surprised if it was all jus' a trick to get that knife. She knew we'd got that knife an' she cut those branches off with you there jus' to make you think she wanted it done an' bring the knife to do it, and then when you did she sprang out at you an' got the knife. I shun't be a bit surprised if it was that that happened."

This sinister aspect of the affair greatly appealed to Ginger.

"I think so, too," he said. "Why should she cut off branches herself an' then go on at me for cuttin' them off, if it wasn't? At first I thought she'd jus' gone mad, but now I think it was jus' a way of gettin' the knife."

"It was jolly clever," conceded William grudgingly, "but we're goin' to be a jolly sight cleverer gettin' it back. Let's think out a way."

"It's no good me goin' to her," said Ginger hastily, "she'll only go ravin' mad again if she sees me, an' start shakin' my head off again. It's not myself I'm thinkin' of," he added, "it's her. I don't want her to get hung for murder same as she would if she killed me. I'm not frightened of her. It's only I don't want her to get hung for murder."

"Well, anyway it's not much good you goin'," agreed William, resisting the temptation to take up the challenge. "She knows you, an' she's mad at you, an' she wouldn't give you back the knife whatever you did. No, I'd better go. She's never seen me. I'll wait till to-morrow mornin'. She may've begun to feel sorry in the night. Sometimes people do. She may've jus' been in a rage an' want to make up for it. I'll plead an' reason with her first, an' give her a chance to be decent, an' then if she won't be we'll have to think out a plan."

So the next morning William set off alone to Aunt Amelia's cottage. There was no one in the garden, and, with trepidation at his heart, William walked up the path and knocked at the cottage door.

A woman with short straight grey hair, wearing horn-rimmed spectacles and a soulful expression, opened it. Now William had not seen Ginger's aunt, and it never occurred to him that this was not she. He could not know, of course, that Ginger's aunt had gone out to do some shopping, and that this was the literary friend. Nor could he know that the literary friend was expecting a child interviewer—the son of an enterprising woman editor who was featuring a series of interviews of famous writers of children's books by children, or, to be precise, by her own child. The child was a highbrow boy of eleven whose efforts, especially after the maternal touchings up, read extremely well.

William, his mind and body poised for instant flight, was unprepared for the beaming smile of welcome with which he was greeted.

"Come in, dear boy," said the literary friend, throwing the door wide and holding out both hands to clasp his. "This is a treat, indeed! How splendid of you to get here so early! Come into my little sanctum. I allow very few people in my little sanctum, but you, of course, will be an honoured guest."

The bewildered William followed her into the sanctum. Her conscience must have been troubling her in the night. Or else Ginger had utterly misjudged her. Or else she was mad as Ginger had suggested, and with the cunning of the insane she was luring him into her parlour in order to be able to shake his head off in comfort. He sat down guardedly upon the edge of a chair and stared at her blankly.

"Now, dear," said the literary friend brightly, "before we talk about what you've come here to talk about, let's get to know each other. I want you to call me Flavia. That's the name all my writing friends call me by, and you're one of my writing friends, you know. I think you write so well, dear boy. I did so much enjoy that last thing of yours."

William was touched and gratified. He was aware that

"COME IN, DEAR BOY," SAID THE LITERARY FRIEND. "HOW
SPLENDID OF YOU TO GET HERE SO EARLY!"

Ginger possessed a copy of his story "Dick of the Bloody Hand," but he did not know that he had shown it to his aunt. The fact that she had evidently been able to read it was an additional source of gratification to him, for it had been copied out hastily by William himself and was considered by most people—unjustly, as William thought—to be utterly illegible.

He smiled self-consciously.

"Oh, well," he said, "I'm glad you liked it."

"Of *course* I liked it, dear boy," gushed Flavia. "Now I do so want to get to know you, dear boy; really to *know* you."

The literary friend was determined to make a conquest of the youthful interviewer. She was hoping great things from the interview, and she knew that a lot depended on what impression she made on the boy who was to write it.

"Now, dear boy, tell me some of the fancies and imaginings that go on in your clever little head."

William gaped at her.

"The what?" he said.

"The things you pretend to yourself, dear boy. Ah, I'm sure that you live in a world of make-believe."

"Oh, yes," said William. "Yes, I do often pretend things. I often pretend I'm a cannibal cookin' people, or a pirate makin' people walk the plank, or a prehistoric monster crunchin' human bones."

Flavia winced and paled.

"Y-yes," she said. "Well, now, suppose that we talk of what you've come here to talk to me about."

"Yes," said William eagerly. He felt much encouraged by the tone of the interview, but he was aware that even so he must go carefully. He decided to lead up to the subject of the knife slowly and gradually.

"You like my little boykins?" went on Flavia coyly.

William thought this an odd way of referring to
Ginger, but there was no doubt at all that Ginger's aunt
was a very odd person.

"Oh, yes," he said, "I'm his greatest friend."

"How *sweet* of you to say that!" purred Flavia.

"Yes," said William, "an' he *means* to help. He
really does mean to help."

"But he *does* help, dear boy," said Flavia reproachfully. "He brings sunshine and happiness into the lives
of everyone around him."

William's bewilderment increased. Never had an
interview run on more unexpected lines.

"Y-yes," said William. "Yes, I think that he does,
too. He doesn't know much about gard'nin' p'raps, an'
p'raps he makes some mistakes—"

"But he *does* know about gardening," said Flavia
rather indignantly; "he's *devoted* to gardening. And he
doesn't make mistakes. . . . He's got one of those sweet
child souls that are born with a sort of *understanding* of
Nature."

William blinked helplessly, then made another gallant
effort. "He understands other flowers, of course," he
said, "but he doesn't understand *roses* very well. He
doesn't know when to chop 'em off, but he wants to
learn. He—"

"*Roses!*" ejaculated Flavia. "But, my dear boy,
surely you remember the rose garden he made and
tended with his own hands for the bedridden old lady—
made it where she could see it from her bed—and came
to look after it and cut its blooms for her every
afternoon. She liked a particular copper-coloured rose,
you remember, and he took a lot of trouble growing it
for her."

William struggled against an overmastering feeling of
unreality.

"Not Ginger," he said weakly.

"I didn't say ginger," snapped Flavia, losing her poise for a moment; "there isn't such a thing as a ginger rose. I said copper-coloured."

William tried unavailingly to reconcile this anecdote with what he knew of the history and character of Ginger.

"I don't remember jus' that," he said at last. "I remember once we found a dead cat an' we stuck it up in old General Moult's rose bed to make him come runnin' down to scare it off, an' he did an'—"

Flavia had risen with an abrupt movement. She had herself well under control, however. She remembered that in the hands of this coarse and objectionable boy lay her reputation, as far as the interview was concerned. She had taken a paper from a drawer and was thrusting it into his hands.

"I think that if you will incorporate this in the article, dear boy," she said, fixing a glassy smile on him, "I needn't detain you any longer. It's a short summary of my aims and ideals. And I had a little present for you." She stopped and considered. It would never do to give this boy the present that she had purchased for the interviewer—a charming little picture called Flower Fairies. For a second she stood frowning uncertainly. She wanted to give the boy some present that would appeal to him and make him feel inclined to extol her in his account of the interview. However uncouth he seemed, he had written some quite good articles on the writers of children's books and his praise was worth something. Suddenly her face cleared, and she went from the room, returning in a few minutes with something in her hand that made William's eyes gleam.

"Take this, dear boy," she said. "It belonged to a tiresome, destructive child who maimed some of the beautiful things of Nature with it. I'm sure you'll make better use of it."

Speechless with amazement, bewilderment, and joy, William snatched the knife and, murmuring incoherent thanks, departed with it abruptly, running as fast as he could to the old barn where Ginger awaited him.

"Well?" said Ginger eagerly.

"Got it," said William breathlessly, brandishing his booty.

"How did you get it? Did you plead with her?" said Ginger.

William stood, his mind going silently back over the curious interview that had culminated in the recovery of the knife.

"She *is* mad," he said at last solemnly; "she didn't say one single word of sense all the time we were talkin'. She said you'd made a rose out of copper for an old woman."

"*Me?*" said Ginger.

"Yes. She was ravin' like that all the time. An' she gave me these papers. . . ."

William took the sheaf of neatly written paper from his pocket and together he and Ginger studied it. It contained such words as "atmosphere", "execution", and "technique", used in wholly unintelligible connections.

"*Mad!*" said William again in an awestruck voice. "*Course* she's mad. This proves it. She had a mad look in her eye, too. Talkin' about people makin' roses out of coppers. An' all these pages an' pages of ravin'."

"Anyway, we've got the knife back," said Ginger.

"Yes, an' I'm lucky to get out without her murderin' me. There she was ravin' away as mad as mad, an' then she went and got the knife. I bet you anythin' she got it to murder me with, but I was too quick for her." A faraway look came into William's eyes as he readjusted his memories till he distinctly recalled a blood-curdling struggle with the mad woman for the possession of the knife. "Yes, I was jus' too quick for her, snatchin' it from her hand jus' before she plunged it into me. I ought to have it for a fortnight for that."

"All right, you can," said Ginger. "I feel I've had enough of it to last me more than a fortnight."

He had taken up the carefully written script and was studying it again.

"Fancy her writin' all this stuff, wastin' good paper!"

"We won't waste it," said William. "Let's make it into paper boats, an' have a race on the stream with them."

*   *   *

Ginger's aunt had returned from her shopping expedition. She laid her parcels on the hat-stand and peeped into the literary friend's sanctum.

"I suppose he's not been yet, dear, has he?" she said eagerly.

The literary friend was sitting at her desk, her head on her hands. She raised a haggard face.

"Yes, dear, he's been," she said brokenly. "He's been, and never have I ever seen a child so utterly, *utterly* devoid of spiritual fragrance. He hadn't the most elementary appreciation of art. He hadn't the faintest conception of the meaning of the word literature. The delicacy, the *atmosphere* of my work meant nothing to him. I've given him my notes for the interview, but they'll convey nothing to him. *Nothing*."

Aunt Amelia's eyes were fixed upon the garden gate.

"Who's that?" she said.

A boy was coming in at the garden gate. He carried an attaché case and wore gloves and spectacles. He looked pale and aesthetic and intellectual. He exuded spiritual

fragrance from every pore. Behind him, beaming
maternal pride, came a woman whom Flavia recognised
as the editress of the journal.

Aunt Amelia and the literary friend stared at them in
helpless bewilderment. . . .

Chapter 6

William and the Watch and Chain

William and Robert were at present on fairly friendly terms. William found this state of things rather dull on the whole, despite his mother's frequent discourses on the Happiness of Living Together in Unity. He was, however, taking a good deal of trouble to preserve the peace, not from any love of peace for its own sake—he found a state of feud far more stimulating and exciting—but because Christmas was only a week ahead and he had learnt to tread very warily in the vicinity of the festival. Experience had taught him that the monetary value of people's presents to you depends very much on the relations that happen to exist between you and them at the time. On one occasion Robert had given him no present at all because he had taken his, Robert's, bicycle to pieces to see how it was made, and, putting it together again, had omitted a vital part.

He had learnt, too, that the general state of the giver's affairs—quite apart from their pecuniary aspect—has a great effect upon the value of the gift. One whose affairs are running smoothly is more inclined to be generous than one whose affairs are awry. Therefore, he was watching Robert's affairs carefully. For Robert's Christmas present to him this year was very important. Their father was giving Robert a new watch, and Robert had hinted that he might give William his old watch for a Christmas present.

Though time mattered little enough to William, he was anxious to possess a watch and chain, and Robert's was a large, important-looking watch with a thick silver chain. It was a watch and chain that would considerably increase William's prestige among his contemporaries. And so he trod warily with Robert and watched over his affairs with an anxious eye. Robert's chief affair was, needless to say, an affair of the heart, for Robert was notoriously susceptible to feminine charm. His present inamorata was a damsel with ash blonde hair and violet eyes called Honoria Mercer, whose family had recently come to live in the village. Experience had taught William that efforts to help affairs of that sort recoil very frequently upon their author's head, so he contented himself by avoiding Honoria as far as possible, but behaving with unexampled politeness whenever a meeting was inevitable. This mode of procedure was startlingly successful—so much so that Honoria one day remarked innocently to Robert: "What a nice, polite little boy your brother is."

Robert was so staggered by this remark that he remained open-mouthed and silent for several minutes, but William, hearing of it, felt that his chances of the watch and chain were perceptibly increased.

*   *   *

The usual Christmas festivities were afoot. The Browns were giving a party the day before Christmas Eve, and the week after Christmas the Botts were giving a large fancy dress dance.

William's whole attention was divided between the watch and chain and the fancy dress dance. A school friend, who could not go to the dance, had lent William his costume—that of a pantomime cat. It was a gorgeous affair with a large, grinning head, whiskers, and a furry body that buttoned up the front. William had secreted the costume in his room without telling anyone what it was. To William the essence of success of a fancy dress costume lay in its secrecy. The thought of prancing about among the guests in his cat costume, playing whatever tricks he pleased, without anyone's guessing his identity, was a very enjoyable one. The whole thing would be spoilt for him if people knew who he was. Unfortunately Ethel had seen the tail hanging out of the parcel as he carried it upstairs, and so the family knew that he was to go as an animal of some sort, but more than that he would not tell them. He hoped that there would be so many other animals that his own identity would not be guessed. He kept the drawer in which he had put it locked, and assumed a cunning, sphinx-like air when any of his family asked him about it.

The question of the watch and chain, however, was the question that loomed largest on his mental horizon.

He had made up his mind to obliterate himself as far as possible on the day of his own family's party so as not to prejudice his chances of the precious gift. In any case it was Robert's and Ethel's party and sure to be dull. They were to have charades after supper—a decision that made William snort contemptuously.

"Why not have a real *game*," he said, "like 'Tigers and Tamers', or something excitin' like that? Just dressin' up! Huh!"

* * *

Honoria was the last guest to arrive, and Robert at once took her under his care with an *empressement* that William secretly found highly amusing. He controlled his mirth, however, contenting himself with a mental mimicry of Robert's manner that gave him much inward satisfaction. He had not looked forward to the party, but his spirits rose as he entered the dining-room at the tail of the guests. He had not been allowed to take any part in these preparations, and he was much impressed by the scale of magnificence on which they had been made. He remembered, however, that his behaviour on this occasion might vitally affect his possession or non-possession of the silver watch and so he refused food himself with stoical endurance and plied Honoria with provisions till she felt almost embarrassed by his attentions. He made up for the self-restraint this imposed by staying behind in the dining-room when everyone else had gone into the drawing-room. He even followed the feast into the kitchen and stayed there, finishing up everything within reach, till the cook drove him away.

On his return to the drawing-room he found the game of charades just beginning. One side had been chosen to act, the other side to watch. Robert and Honoria were on the watching side and promptly withdrew to the morning-room to wait till the charade was ready to begin. Robert did not believe in wasting time. . . . William was on the acting side, and he accompanied the others into the hall, beginning to feel excited despite himself. He had thoughtfully filled his pockets with chocolate biscuits and munched them busily as the others discussed what word to act.

Occasionally he made a suggestion, but as no one took any notice of it he finally gave his whole attention to the chocolate biscuits. Suddenly he discovered that Ethel was addressing him. . . . Ethel, it appeared, was to represent the Queen of Sheba, and William was to be her slave.

"Go and put on my happi coat, William," she said. "It's hanging behind the door. You can hitch it up at the waist if it's too long, and you'll find a scarf in my top drawer that you can make into a turban."

William obeyed these orders zestfully. He secretly enjoyed dressing up, though he pretended to despise it. The effect of the happi coat and scarf-turban was certainly impressive. But there was something missing. He had once seen a picture of the Queen of Sheba with a page in attendance and the page had been black. Yes, he certainly ought to be black. His face at any rate. . . . He came downstairs to the hall to consult someone, but it was empty. The actors were all changing in various bedrooms. Screams of laughter came from his mother's bedroom where Ethel and her friends were dressing. . . . He wondered whether to go and ask Ethel, then decided not to in case she said it wasn't necessary. No, best confront them with a face already blackened: they couldn't very well tell him to go and take it off then. The next question was how to get the blacking. It would be useless to go to the kitchen and ask for it. The cook had already chased him out in fury. He decided to creep out into the garden by the side door, go round to the back of the house and get the blacking through the pantry window. He'd put the blacking on his face outside in the garden to prevent all possibility of anyone's seeing him and telling him not to, and on the way back he'd just look in at the morning-room window to see how Robert was getting on with Honoria. It was very important to him that Robert should get on well with Honoria and so be in a good temper—and consequently generously inclined—on Christmas day.

*   *   *

Robert was finding Honoria rather heavy going, but this did not in any way decrease his fervour. On the other hand it rather increased it, for Robert, true to his race, found difficulty a stimulant, not a deterrent. Honoria seemed bent on discussing her favourite masculine qualities, which seemed a promising enough topic in the circumstances, but, despite all Robert's efforts, she refused to pass from the general to the particular.

"What I really admire *most* in a man," said Honoria fervently, "is courage."

Robert assumed a modest air.

"I'm told," he said casually, "that I once met a bull in a field when I was little more than a child and showed no fear at all."

"I expect you thought it was a cow," said Honoria carelessly, and continued: "Courage is a quality that seems to be dying out among modern men. I mean, you've only got to read historical novels to see that. The things they do in historical novels! Really *brave* things, I mean. Well, I don't know a single modern man who would do the things people do quite as a matter of course in historical novels. I mean, they'll fight whole crowds of people and get wounded all over and then they'll run away so fast that no one can catch them, and then they'll fight more men and escape out of prison, climbing down rocks and jumping over precipices and that sort of thing—and I've just read one where the man's attacked by a whole pack of savage bloodhounds and strangles them every one, and then climbs right up the outside of a high tower to rescue the girl who's imprisoned there. . . ."

Robert cast his eyes back over the nineteen years of his life, but could think of no exploits to compete with that.

"It sounds like something on the pictures," he said coldly.

"Oh, the pictures!" she said contemptuously. "All the things you see on the pictures are faked, you know.

Dummies and things. They don't thrill me in the least. No, it's real courage in real life that thrills me, and there simply doesn't seem to be any of it left. . . ."

"I've got a little car, you know," said Robert, trying to change the subject; "it's just one of those baby things but I can touch sixty on her quite easily."

Honoria shook her ash blonde head sadly.

"There's no *bravery* in that," she said.

"I know," said Robert; "I never said there was. I was just telling you. I thought it possible that you'd be interested."

"No," said Honoria, "I'm not interested in cars. I don't know why. They simply don't thrill me."

"I was playing rugger the other day," said Robert modestly, "and I got two goals and a try all within half an hour. They were the only goals anyone got all through the game. There were a lot of people watching. I felt quite embarrassed when they cheered. . . ."

But the violet blue eyes remained dreamy and aloof.

"Games don't thrill me either," said Honoria. "Not at all. I don't know why. It's the way I'm made, I suppose. It's *courage* that thrills me, not just *strength*. . . . You know, I once heard of a man and he was alone in the house and he saw a perfectly *dreadful* face looking in at him through the window, and without a moment's hesitation he smashed the window and—"

Robert had turned instinctively to the window and there met the blackened face of William. He did not recognise William, and certainly the face as a face was terrifying enough, the whites of the eyes showing up horribly against the shining blackness. Robert sprang up with a yell of terror and plunged towards the door. Honoria, too, had turned to the window, but William had by now disappeared.

"What on earth's the matter?" said Honoria.

ROBERT SPRANG UP WITH A YELL OF TERROR AND PLUNGED
TOWARDS THE DOOR.

"A face!" gasped Robert. "There was a most *ghastly*
face at the window."

Honoria gave him an icy glance from her violet blue
eyes, then swept from the room without a word.

Explanations, of course, only made the situation
worse. For William, standing in the full light of the hall,
looked a harmless enough object, despite his blackened
face.

"And anyway," said Honoria distantly, "even if
there had been danger—well, to run away yourself and
leave me there—!"

Words failed her. . . . She gave him another douche
of violet blue ice and turned away.

For the rest of the evening she ignored him completely, devoting herself to his friend and rival, Jameson Jameson, whom hitherto she had treated with indifference.

Robert managed to obtain a short interview with her before she went home. . . . In it he passionately protested his courage and devotion, and offered to do any deed of daring she chose to name in order to prove his mettle, but it was useless.

"No," she said, "I'm sorry, but I'm like that. I simply can't forgive cowardice."

"But you don't understand," pleaded Robert. "I'll do anything . . . *anything*. Honestly. I'm not a coward. Ask anyone who knows me. . . ."

"I prefer to trust my own eyes," said Honoria icily, and left him protesting passionately to the empty air.

He lost no time in blaming William for the state of affairs, and William in his turn protested passionately, but in vain.

"How was I to *know?*" he said. "I was jus' lookin' in as I was passin'. Well, there's no lor against jus' lookin' in at a window as you're passin', is there? I didn't mean to do any harm."

"Terrifying her like that!" said Robert fiercely—for Robert, of course, had not given William quite a true account of the affair. "Naturally she doesn't want to have anything more to do with a man whose brother goes about playing tricks of that sort."

William, who hoped still to possess the watch and chain despite this contretemps, behaved with unexampled meekness, but Robert's wrath did not abate. During the evening, when someone mentioned that he was to have a gold watch for his Christmas present, Mrs. Brown said:

"And you're going to give your old one to William,

aren't you, dear?"

Whereupon Robert snorted sardonically and said:

"No. I should jolly well think I'm not. I'm going to sell it."

During the next day William tried hard to think of some way of overcoming Robert's anger and so obtaining the watch and chain on which his heart was set, but no plan occurred to him. Probably, of course, if he saved Robert's life Robert might melt towards him and give him the watch and chain, but short of that he could think of nothing to meet the situation.

A fair had come to the village, and the Browns had decided to pay it a visit on Christmas Eve. They all set off together, Robert and William ignoring each other completely. Robert secretly felt a little nervous. He knew that William regarded himself as unfairly treated in the matter of the watch and chain, and, though determined not to give it to him, he was prepared for reprisals.

William did not as a rule accept unfair treatment without retaliation, and, glancing at his freckled, expressionless face, Robert suspected that even now he was evolving some plan of revenge.

On reaching the fair ground the first people they met were Jameson Jameson and Honoria. Jameson Jameson gave them a sheepish grin and Honoria pretended not to see them. Robert ground his teeth and threw a furious glance at William. William maintained his impassive demeanour and as soon as possible escaped from his family to wander round the fair ground himself and drown his troubles in Aunt Sally and Houp-la, and brandy snaps and coconuts. . . . The rest of the family also wandered off, and Robert was left alone, leaning morosely against the support of a booth. He could see Jameson Jameson and Honoria . . . they had just descended from the roundabout and were standing engrossed in animated and very amicable conversation near him, but still ignoring him. Honoria's scorn of him had made her all the more desirable in his eyes, and his misery and sense of desolation were almost unbearable.

Suddenly, to his amazement, a large, shaggy head appeared round the corner of the booth, and he found himself gazing into what was apparently the face of a lion. . . . The vague suspicions of William that had been smouldering in his heart all day sprang to life in a second. He remembered the fancy dress costume—"some sort of animal"—that William had kept so secret. This, then, was the trick the kid had been planning . . . to dress up in his costume and try to expose him in public as a coward—a point on which he was just now so peculiarly sensitive.

He made a threatening gesture at the face.

"Get off with you," he said. "I know who you are and I've had enough of your tricks."

The creature receded a few steps. Robert followed it. His anger now was beyond control. He'd *show* the kid!

"Go straight home," he said, "and take that thing off, and I'll jolly well give you something to think of instead of monkey tricks like this. . . ."

The creature backed before him, and Robert followed it, still with threatening words and gestures. So inflamed was he with fury that he did not see people fleeing on all sides, climbing the tent-poles, barricading themselves in the caravans.

Across the open fair ground backed the lion, followed threateningly by Robert, the scene watched with breathless terror by the spectators from their hiding-places. Then suddenly Robert saw something that turned his blood to ice. He saw William watching the scene from the doorway of a tent, a piece of coconut in one hand, a brandy snap in the other, his mouth open wide with amazement. But before Robert, realising suddenly the true state of affairs, could turn to flee, two men had come up, secured the animal with ropes, and were leading it off. Turning round, dazed and trembling, Robert saw Jameson Jameson adorning the top of the flag-pole, while Honoria stood at the bottom of it, her hands clasped, her eyes, alight with hero-worship, fixed ardently upon Robert.

The spectators rushed from their hiding-places and crowded round Robert, congratulating, praising. He had recovered himself quickly.

"Oh, that's nothing," he said lightly. "It's simply that I never have been frightened of lions. They simply don't frighten me."

He brushed them aside and made his way to where Honoria still stood, gazing at him in ardent admiration.

"Oh, can you ever forgive me for doubting you?" she said.

"Of course, of course," said Robert, generously. "Don't mention it."

"When I saw the awful creature standing there and *him*"—with a scornful glance at Jameson, who was slowly and ungracefully descending his flag-pole—"getting up that thing and not caring whether I was eaten alive or not, and *you* . . . Oh, I've never seen anything so *brave* in all my life!"

Robert straightened his tie with a modest, deprecating gesture.

"Oh, that's nothing," he said. "I'm simply not frightened of lions, that's all. As a matter of fact, I'm not frightened of anything. I was just having a little joke on you the other night, pretending to be frightened. I'd no idea you were going to take it seriously. . . ."

"I can see now how stupid it was of me," she said. "You *do* forgive me, don't you?"

"I'VE NEVER SEEN ANYTHING SO *BRAVE* IN ALL MY LIFE!"
HONORIA EXCLAIMED.

"Of course," said Robert.

Someone came up and reported that the keepers had said that it was very plucky of Robert to tackle the beast, as it had a very uncertain temper.

"Oh, I could see that," said Robert. "That was the first thing I noticed. I thought: 'The beast's got a very uncertain temper. I'd better get him back to his cage as quickly as possible, or he'll be doing some harm. . . .'"

"Oh, how brave of you," said Honoria again, fervently. "Let's get out of the crowd; I'm sure you're tired."

"Oh, no," said Robert, "not a bit. There's nothing in what I did. I'm simply not afraid, that's all. As a matter of fact," he admitted, "I don't know the meaning of the word fear."

"I think you're *wonderful*," breathed Honoria once more.

Jameson Jameson came up to them, looking rather sheepish.

"Congratulations, Robert," he said, and to Honoria: "I say, I'm frightfully sorry. I want to explain. I—"

But it was his turn for a douche of violet blue ice. Honoria turned on her heel and left him, drawing Robert with her.

"The *coward*!" she said between her teeth. "Oh, the *coward*!"

"You mustn't blame him too much," said Robert magnanimously. "After all, some chaps can't *help* being afraid of danger, you know."

"Oh, never mind him. Now tell me everything you thought and felt when you did it."

"Well," said Robert, "the first thing I thought of when I saw it was you. I thought: 'I must get this beast back to its cage before it attacks Honoria. I must defend her from it and if it kills me—well, it won't matter very much after all now that she doesn't believe in me any longer.'"

"Oh, *Robert*!. . . . Robert, will you *ever* forgive me for doubting you? I *know* now that you're the bravest man in the world."

"Oh, well," said Robert modestly, "I shouldn't put it

quite like that."

"I should," persisted Honoria. "It was—oh, it was simply *heroic*."

They were passing the open door of the tent where William stood watching them, still transfixed by amazement. Robert felt generously inclined. Moreover, he realised that indirectly he owed his good fortune to William.

He took off his watch and chain and slipped them carelessly into William's hands as he passed. . . .

Chapter 7

William's Wonderful Plan

William noticed the caravan the first morning it appeared and formed his plans at once for acquaintance with its owners. Caravans had a peculiar fascination for William. He had always found in caravan dwellers, whether of gypsy or Bohemian persuasion, a pleasing freedom from the conventions and prejudices of regular householders. Nobody expected you to wipe your feet on entering a caravan. You were not received by an immaculate and disapproving housemaid. Your way was not barred at every turn by collapsible tables covered with breakable ornaments. The enjoyment of food was not curtailed by a host of mysterious taboos. Nobody minded your speaking with your mouth full in a caravan. You needn't begin with bread and butter. You could put your elbows on the table, which was probably a packing-case, and tip up your chair, which was probably a petrol tin. Caravan life, in fact, was a perpetual picnic. It was an unending source of surprise to William that anyone lived in a house who could possibly live in a caravan.

Immediately after school he made his way down to the caravan and hung about it, pretending to be absorbed in examining the hedges, but in reality surveying the land. He had learnt caution in his eleven years' experience of life. It didn't do to draw conclusions too rashly. The unexpected often happened. Even a caravan might contain that ancient and unrelenting enemy of William's, a "house-proud" woman.

He could see a man in the next field seated at an easel, painting. He had a brown, pointed beard and wore an overall. He looked satisfactorily vague—the sort of man who would never notice that a small boy had miraculously attached himself to the caravan party. With luck, of course, he might be camping with another man just like himself. With greater luck he might be camping alone. There were, of course, women so vague that they accepted a small boy's presence at meals as a matter of course and without question, but they were few and far between. . . . William was just about to draw closer to the caravan in order to peep cautiously through the open door, when a little girl appeared suddenly in the doorway. She was about William's age, with a round, dimpled face and dark curls. William, at her appearance, had hastily begun to busy himself in the hedge.

"What are you doing there, boy?" said the little girl in a clear voice.

"Nothin'," said William shortly, still pretending to examine the hedge with deep interest and, though answering her question, trying to look wholly unaware of her presence.

"Are you looking for birds' nests?"

"Uh-huh," said William non-committally.

"Well, stop doing, and come and help me wash up."

Impressed despite himself by the imperiousness of the little girl's voice, William yet managed to preserve his manly independence so far as to reply:

"Can't. I'm busy."

"That's not being busy," said the little girl indignantly. "Standing and staring at a hedge isn't being

"STARING AT A HEDGE ISN'T BEING BUSY," SAID THE GIRL.
"COME AND HELP ME WASH UP."

busy. Come and help me wash up."

"She needn't try bossing me 'cause I'm jolly well not
goin' to be bossed by any ole girl," said William to the
hedge, with a swaggering laugh, but, even as he said it,
he was turning to make his way meekly to the caravan

and within a few minutes was engaged in washing up and sweeping out the tiny room under the little girl's orders.

She informed him, while he did so, that she had had measles, and that this caravan holiday with her father was her final convalescence before she returned to school.

"My father," she informed him simply, "is the greatest artist in the world. He can cook, too, but he's very untidy. If I wasn't here the place would be a pigsty." And she bustled about, dusting, tidying, putting away the tea-things. . . .

She was certainly not William's ideal caravan dweller. On the other hand, her dimples were distinctly attractive, and, despite the manly independence of which he so frequently boasted, William found her imperious manner distinctly intriguing.

His mother was pleased at the speed with which he set off to school the next morning and much surprised to hear that he had been late. His explanation that he had got lost on the way was unconvincing. In reality, he had, at the little girl's bidding, washed up the caravaners' breakfast things (the artist was already at work in the next field), and dusted and swept out the caravan.

After that he called there regularly on his way to school, and spent most of his dinner-hour and evening there. Although he liked to imagine himself a world potentate at whose bidding thousands trembled, he had already become the little girl's willing slave. It gave him a strange pleasure to obey the imperious little voice, it thrilled him to his very soul to clean the small brown strap-over shoes, as he did now every morning. His waking dreams took the form of heroic exploits in which he rescued her from bulls and runaway horses and motor-cars out of control and bands of Red Indians. His chief quarrel with life was that it gave him no opportunity for those feats. His friends would have been surprised at the humility with which the world potentate received the little girl's curt orders, and the meekness with which the scorner of civilisation swept and scoured and dusted the caravan. For the little girl was notably devoid of that spirit of *laissez-faire* that William considered the essential of a perfect caravan dweller. . . .

She refused all William's efforts to beguile her into the larger life of the fields and woods.

"We could play Red Indians," he said wistfully, "and you could be my squaw."

"Oh, but I think it much more fun playing house like this, don't you?" said the little girl, who was engaged in cleaning the spoons and forks.

"Yes," said the shorn Samson, industriously sweeping the caravan's only carpet.

The artist addressed him as "boy" whenever he met him, and seemed to feel no interest or curiosity about him, never asking where he came from or what he was doing in the caravan. Instead he held forth to him upon abstruse questions of art, brandishing his palette and striding to and fro as he talked.

Like William, he was the little girl's slave, obeying her orders and allowing her to mother and scold him to her heart's content.

William, aware that in the eyes of the world his subjection to his goddess would seem unworthy if not ridiculous, had told no one about the caravan and its occupants, but he soon found that the news had spread through the village.

Mrs. Bott, of the Hall, coming to invite William to a children's garden party, added: "And I'm going to ask that little girl who's camping here with her father. He's quite distinguished, I hear. An R.A. and all that. . . ."

When Mrs. Bott had gone, William, who hated visits

to the Hall, did his best to extricate himself from the festivity.

"I'm sure I shan't be well enough," he pleaded to his mother. "It's no good me goin' there with an illness comin' on an givin' it to everyone there."

"But you haven't got an illness, William," protested his mother.

"I din' say I had got one jus' this minute," said William. "I only said I felt I was goin' to have one that afternoon. I mean, it doesn't seem fair to people to say you'll go to a place when you *know* you're only goin' to give them all an illness."

"If you think you're going to be ill, William, I'll ask the doctor to call."

William hastily retreated from his position.

"No, I din' mean that. What I meant was that it would be *kinder* of me not to go. I mean, if I don' go she'll have one less to feed an' look after and so on. I think it would be selfish of me to give her extra trouble by goin' to the party."

"But, William, if everyone thought that there'd be no party at all."

"An' a jolly good thing!" said William feelingly.

But he saw that protest would be unavailing and that on the day of the garden party he would be scrubbed and brushed and despatched to the Hall with other youthful merrymakers.

"If you aren't well on the day," said his mother, "we'll send for the doctor, of course."

"Oh, will you?" said William with a sinister laugh. "I'd rather go to the beastly party than be poisoned by his stuff."

"You'll probably enjoy yourself, William."

"Enjoy myself!" exploded William. "Yes, they say 'enjoy yourself' one minute, an' 'don't get rough' the

next. The second you *start* enjoying yourself, they say
'don't get rough' an' take you away from the only people
you can enjoy yourself with, to look after a soppy girl.
How *can* you enjoy yourself without getting rough,
that's what I want to know?"

"People do, you know, William," said Mrs. Brown
mildly.

"No, they don't," said William. "They think they do,
but they don't. You *can't* enjoy yourself without gettin'
rough. It stands to reason you can't."

But, as far as William himself was concerned, he had
given up the struggle. He knew that he would be
compelled either to go to Mrs. Bott's children's garden
party, or swallow one of the doctor's nauseous draughts,
and of the two he preferred the former fate. But his
thoughts flew protectively to the little girl. From his
garnered stores of wisdom he would teach her how to
escape the ordeal. A father alone must be easy enough
to manage. He would impart to her, under oath of
secrecy, some of those "symptoms" that, before time
had dulled their use, had deceived even that Argus-eyed
lynx, William's family doctor.

But, to his surprise, the little girl impatiently waved
aside his advice.

"Don't be silly, William," she said. "I *want* to go. Of
course I want to go. It's a *party*. The only thing—"

She sighed and the sparkle died away from her face.

"Yes?" said William.

"I haven't got a proper party dress. . . . I've just got
an old muslin one all washed out and ever so much too
short. . . . And all the others will have lovely dresses. I
shan't enjoy it a bit. . . ."

"Well, don't go then," said William.

She stamped her small foot. "Don't be *silly*. I tell you
I *want* to go."

"Well, ask your father to get you a new dress."

"No, I won't. He's poor and he's working hard and he mustn't be worried. You see, the one I have does all right for school, but it'll look *awful* at a garden party, because I *know* all the others will have nicer ones."

William could not bear the sight of the downcast little face, its dimples fled.

"Now, look here," he said impulsively, "don't you worry. Don't you worry a single *minute*. I'll see that you have a nice party dress for it."

He was aghast when he heard himself make this astounding offer, but it was too late to retract. Her face beamed with joy. The dimples had returned to it. . . .

"Oh, William! Will you *really*!"

He found her gratitude very pleasing. He assumed an attitude of manly omnipotence.

"'Course I will," he said with a short laugh. "A little thing like that's nothin' to me. Nothin' at all."

Suddenly the dimples fled again.

"William, you mustn't let anyone know you're getting it for me, will you? I should feel like a beggar if you did."

William gave another short laugh into which, despite himself, something of dismay had crept.

"Oh, no," he said. "'Course I wouldn't do that. Good gracious, no. . . . No, I'll get you a jolly nice new party dress, a jolly nice new one. You needn't worry about *that*."

The little girl beamed once more.

"Oh, William!" she said, "you are wonderful. Go an' get it now *quickly*."

William walked away, trying to make his back view still convey the impression of careless omnipotence. His face, however, which the little girl could not see, registered the deepest consternation. He could not think

how he had come to make such a wildly impossible offer.
Moreover, his promise not to tell anyone why he wanted
the party frock, complicated matters still further. . . .
William, however, never abandoned an undertaking
because it seemed hopeless. He approached his mother
first of all.

"Mother," he said thoughtfully that evening. "I
don't mind goin' to this party of Mrs. Bott's if I can go in
fancy dress."

"But of *course* you can't go in fancy dress, William,"
said his mother firmly. "It isn't a fancy dress party."

"How do you know it isn't?" said William.

"She'd have said if it was."

"P'raps it is, and she forgot to say. Anyway, I think I
ought to have a fancy dress ready 'case it is. I shall look
jolly silly if the day comes an' it's a fancy dress party, an'
I've nothin' to go in."

"But William, what *nonsense*! Why *should* it be a
fancy dress party? And even if it is you've got your Red
Indian suit."

"I'm sick of that ole Red Indian suit. I've worn it at
every fancy dress party I've been to 'cept when I was lent
that cat costume."

"You've only worn it twice."

"Well, that's about all the fancy dress parties I've
ever been to, isn't it?"

"If you don't want to go in it, we can easily make you a
pirate with coloured scarves and things."

"I don't want to go as a pirate, either. I want to go as a
little girl. I want you to buy me a little girl's party dress,
so that if we find it's fancy dress at the last minute I can
go in it."

"William," said Mrs. Brown indignantly, "I never
heard such rubbish! It isn't fancy dress to start with, and,
if it were, of *course* you'd have to go in your Red Indian

suit. Why on *earth*—?" She gazed helplessly at William's uncomely, freckled face with its shock of wiry hair. "You'd look *awful* as a little girl, anyway. I can't think what's come over you!"

"Nothin's come over me," said William with dignity. "Surely I can go to a fancy dress party as a little girl if I want to."

"But there is no fancy dress party," protested Mrs. Brown again.

William considered the question again in silence for a few moments, then said: "Well, will you give me a little girl's party dress and count it my Christmas present?"

"It's months till Christmas and what on earth do you want one for?"

"Jus' to have ready 'case this party turns out to be a fancy dress one."

"Now, William, I've no time to stay here talking nonsense with you like this. I've got the lunch to see to."

And Mrs. Brown briskly put away her darning and bustled into the kitchen, leaving William in gloomy contemplation of his first failure. He was not, however, disheartened. He decided next to approach the six-year-old Violet Elizabeth Bott, in whose honour the garden party was being held.

Violet Elizabeth Bott was the apple of her mother's eye. She was dressed always in the height of juvenile modishness, and had innumerable party frocks of lace or net, fashionably short and frilly. Her hair was a mop of carefully tended golden curls. She had a lisp that her admirers thought adorable. William was not one of her admirers; he considered her "soppy" and avoided her whenever he could. But he thought now wistfully of the endless succession of elaborate frocks in which her small person made its appearance at all the local functions. She was, of course, much smaller than the little girl of the caravan, but surely, thought William, the little girl could make one dress for herself out of two of Violet Elizabeth's, and surely Violet Elizabeth could spare two from her capacious wardrobe. He approached the Hall cautiously and found Violet Elizabeth, wearing a dress of embroidered linen of the latest shade of green, sitting on an upturned wheel-barrow.

"I'm a pwincess, William," she announced. "An' you're my subject. You've got to bow when you speak to me."

Ordinarily, William would have ignored her, but to the lady's gratification and secret surprise he bowed. It was a most ungracious bow, but it was indisputably a bow.

"Look here," he began. "I want to ask you something."

"You must say 'Your Woyal Highness' when you speak to me," said Violet Elizabeth imperiously.

"Your Royal Highness," muttered William. "Look here . . . I want to ask you—"

Violet Elizabeth had leapt from the wheel-barrow.

"I want to go for a wide," she said. "Make my thwone into a chawiot."

William obediently turned over the wheel-barrow.

"Now, look here," he said. "What I want to ask you—"

"Now you're my coachman," said Violet Elizabeth, reposing on the wheel-barrow and arranging her miniature skirt about her with dignity. "Give me a wide, coachman."

Still forcing his proud spirit to this uncongenial servitude, William took up the handles of the wheel-barrow and began to push the small tyrant round the lawn.

"Now, look here," he began again rather breathlessly, "this is what I wanted to ask you—"

"You must say 'Your Woyal Highness' when you speak to me," said Violet Elizabeth. "If you don't I'll have your head chopped off for tweason."

"Your Royal Highness," said William shortly. "Now, this is what I wanted to ask you. I wanted to ask you—"

"Go faster," said Violet Elizabeth. "You're going too slowly. I'm a pwincess an' if you don't go faster I'll have your head chopped off for tweason."

William increased his pace, trying to summon up a vivid memory of the little girl in the caravan in order to steel his spirit to endure this humiliation in her cause.

"I'm having a new fwock from London for our party," announced Violet Elizabeth.

It was a heaven-sent opening.

"That's what I was goin' to ask you," panted William.

"It's goin' to be yellow *cwêpe de Chine*, jus' the colour of my hair," continued Violet Elizabeth complacently.

"I say," said the perspiring William, "you've got lots of party frocks, haven't you?"

"Hundweds an' hundweds, an' say 'Your Woyal Highness' or I'll have you awested for tweason."

"Your Royal Highness—well, now suppose there was another little girl—"

Violet Elizabeth's interest was suddenly aroused.

"Yes," she said. "Go on."

"Suppose there was another little girl that was invited to your party, but had only got a very old frock to come in, wouldn't you want to give her some of your old party frocks that you don't wear any more so that she can have a nice one to come in?"

A seraphic smile appeared upon Violet Elizabeth's angel countenance.

"No, I wouldn't," she said. "I'd *like* her to come in an old fwock, 'cause it would make my new fwock seem smarter than ever."

There was only one thing to do and William did it. He tipped the young autocrat ungently out of the wheel-barrow on to the lawn, then set off himself quickly down the drive. For a second fury and amazement deprived Violet Elizabeth of the power of speech. Then it returned and scream after shrill scream rent the peaceful summer morning.

William turned as he reached the bend in the drive to see Mrs. Bott, Mr. Bott and the whole Bott domestic staff issuing at full speed from the front door in answer to those piercing screams of rage.

William hastened back to his own home, and there, in the shelter of his own back garden, pondered again on the affair. He had not really hoped for much from Violet Elizabeth. Moreover, he felt that he had not quite fulfilled the little girl's condition of secrecy. Perhaps it was as well that he had not succeeded in that quarter. . . . The memory of Violet Elizabeth's undignified descent from the wheel-barrow was a pleasant one and healed all the wounds that his vanity had received in the former part of the interview. Even if Mrs. Bott complained to his mother, he wasn't sorry that he'd done that. . . . Then his thoughts turned again to the question of the little girl's party dress. . . . Something must be done about it. William was not of the stuff that easily acknowledges defeat. He racked his brains unavailingly for some moments, then gradually a light dawned. Last week the Vicar's wife had been to see his mother to ask for her yearly subscription to the Sick and Poor Fund. The little girl was not sick, but she was poor. She had said that they were so poor that her father could not afford to buy her a new party frock. He had himself heard the Vicar's wife say that she had ten pounds in hand for the Sick and Poor Fund, which was a very good record. It would surely not take anything like that to buy the little girl a new party frock. He must approach the Vicar's wife, but he must approach her carefully, more carefully than he had approached Violet Elizabeth. He must not even tell her that it was for a party frock he wanted the money. It would spoil the little girl's pleasure if people knew that her frock had been bought by the Sick and Poor Fund. . . . He set off at once to the Vicarage, but the Vicar's wife was taking a choir practice and could not see him. He called again in the afternoon, but she was holding a raffia class in connection with the Women's Institute and still could not see him. He called again that evening, but she was holding a meeting of Sunday School teachers and still could not see him. It was yet another object lesson to William in the perversity of life in general that, whenever he was engaged on any particularly lawless enterprise, the Vicar's wife would miraculously appear from nowhere and report his activity to his parents, while now, when for the first time in his life he was voluntarily seeking her company, she seemed to be inaccessible. Nothing daunted, he went to see her again the next afternoon.

The Vicar's wife, it appeared, was engaged with a sewing meeting, but as the sewing meeting was nearly over she would see him. . . . She came to him in the study and looked at him sternly.

"Now, William," she said, "if you've broken my cucumber frame again, it's no use asking me not to tell your father. It's my *duty* to tell your father. You've no business to walk round the top of my garden wall the way you do, and if you've fallen down into my cucumber frame again—"

William waved all this aside impatiently.

"It's nothin' to *do* with that," he said. "An' I can walk round *any* wall without fallin' off it. That was *years* ago."

"It was two weeks ago, William," said the Vicar's wife severely. "Well, what have you come about?"

"I've come about the Sick and Poor Fund," said William.

The Vicar's wife stared at him open-mouthed.

"The what?" she said.

"The Sick and Poor Fund," repeated William distinctly. "I want to help you with it."

"You—what?" said the Vicar's wife, still too astounded to believe her ears.

"I want to help you with the Sick an' Poor Fund," said William. He was aware that the path to his demand must be well and truly laid. The Vicar's wife must, of course, be made to believe that he had completely altered his course of life before she would entrust him with the spending of a part of her precious Sick and Poor Fund.

"You see," he went on, "I've quite changed from what I used to be, climbin' trees and walkin' on walls, an' suchlike. I'm beginnin' to take an interest in the sick an' poor an' things like that an' I want to help them. That's why I've come to see you—'cause I want to help the Sick an' Poor Fund. I know you're busy with Sunday Schools an' sewing meetings an' raffia an' suchlike, so I thought p'raps you'd like me to help you with it. With the Sick an' Poor Fund, I mean. You see"—her softening expression was reassuring, and he wanted to remove from her mind all suspicion of ulterior motive on his part—"you see, that's why I've come to see you—jus' 'cause I want to help with this Sick an' Poor Fund."

She was beaming at him.

"This is *very* good news, my dear boy. How much pocket-money do you get?"

It seemed to William a very irrelevant question, but he answered patiently: "Threepence a week"; then went on impatiently: "Now about the Sick an' Poor Fund—"

"Yes, dear boy," said the Vicar's wife, laying a hand affectionately on his head. "Your offer does you the greatest credit. I must say that I'm rather surprised, but it shows that one should never judge others and that there's good in everyone. Now, dear boy, I don't want you to give me *all* your pocket-money, but I think, if you give me three-halfpence a week towards the fund, it will be a most wonderful example to all the other little boys and girls of the village, and it will be a joy to your dear parents and to yourself all your life to think how you helped poor sick people in your childhood."

There came the sound of an opening door and a buzz of voices in the passage outside. The Vicar's wife threw open the study door and faced the members of the sewing meeting with a proud smile, her hand still resting upon the head of the bewildered William.

"Ladies," she said, "this little boy has just been to see me, and I'm sure none of you will guess what he wanted to say to me. He wanted to offer to give me half his pocket-money every week for the Sick and Poor Fund. Don't you think it's a *wonderful* example for a little child to set us all?"

They gazed at William with expressions of petrified amazement. Among them was William's mother, whose face registered not parental pride and gratification, but the deepest anxiety. Either William had suddenly gone mad or she had. . . . She must take his temperature as soon as she got home. Perhaps it was the beginning of brain fever. . . . The others had recovered from their amazement and were congratulating William warmly. William, too astounded to protest, was swept out of the Vicarage front door by the congratulating crowd.

"DON'T YOU THINK IT'S A WONDERFUL EXAMPLE FOR A LITTLE
CHILD TO SET US ALL?" SAID THE VICAR'S WIFE.

THEY GAZED AT WILLIAM WITH EXPRESSIONS OF AMAZEMENT.

"I think I'll arrange with your mother to pay it straight to me, dear boy," the Vicar's wife called after him; "then there will be no temptation to omit the payment. . . ."

At the gate William escaped, and in the refuge of his

own back garden faced the failure of this third attempt to procure a new party frock for the little girl.

He was not worried by the Vicar's wife's misunderstanding of his offer. It would be easy enough to get out of that. He could tell her, for instance, that he had been walking in his sleep and had no memory at all of making the offer. . . . What worried him was the thought of the little girl. Yet, though he hated to confront her with only failure to report, he could not resist the attraction that drew him to her. He set off slowly towards the field.

His mother called him back when he had reached the gate in order to take his temperature. To her surprise it was normal.

She returned to the morning-room and said to her husband, who had just come in: "I'm so worried about William, darling."

"Why? Has he broken another window?"

"Oh, no, darling, nothing like that. But he's been behaving in such an extraordinary manner . . . I mean, first of all this morning he said he wanted to go to a fancy dress party as a little girl!"

"What fancy dress party?"

"None. There isn't one. That makes it so odd. Then this afternoon he goes to the Vicarage and tells Mrs. Monks that he wants to give half his pocket-money every week to the Sick and Poor Fund. His temperature's normal, but do you think that his brain can be going queer?"

Mr. Brown, however, reassured on the score of broken windows, had lost interest in the matter.

"It can't go any queerer than it's always been, if that's any comfort to you," he said, and returned to his evening paper.

Meantime, William was slowly approaching the caravan. He had almost decided frankly to admit failure, but when the little girl came running across the field to him, her eyes bright, her lips parted eagerly, he could not find it in his heart to disappoint her.

"Oh, William," she cried excitedly, when she reached him, "have you got it?"

"Not yet," said William, trying rather unsuccessfully to assume an airy manner. "There's plenty of time."

"There *isn't*, William," she protested.

"There is for *me*," said William. "It'll take me no time to do a little thing like that."

But the little girl was not quite reassured.

"You have got a plan, haven't you, William?" she said anxiously.

He laughed a gay laugh that rang slightly hollow.

"'Course I have," he said. "I should jolly well think so. Catch me not having a plan. I should jolly well think I've got a plan all right."

He was, of course, overdoing his protestations, and she was still looking at him doubtfully.

"You're *sure*?" she said.

"Sure?" repeated William, attempting the gay laugh again, but trying to hide its complete failure by turning it into a cough half-way. "I should jolly well think I am sure."

They had reached the caravan now, and he followed her into it. A much-washed white muslin dress lay over a chair. The little girl took it and held it up.

"It looks *awful*," she said sorrowfully. "I'd rather go in it than not go at all, of course, but I shall feel dreadful if I have to wear it. It's all washed to bits and it's miles too small. But—you *have* promised to get me a new one, haven't you, William?"

"Oh yes," said William with a ghastly smile. "Oh, yes, rather. Oh, yes, don't you worry about that."

"And you really *have* got a plan?"

"Oh, yes," said William. "I've got a plan all right. I should jolly well think I've got a plan all right. . . ."

The church clock struck five. She flung the dress over the chair again.

"That's tea-time. I'll go and fetch father. Be an angel, William, and put on the kettle. The water's in the petrol tin, you know."

She ran off across the field and William, heavy-hearted, lit the spirit kettle as he had seen the little girl do and filled the kettle from the petrol tin. He had often seen the little girl fill the kettle from the petrol tin, but he had never realised that the caravan contained two petrol tins, one full of water, the other of paraffin, and it was from the paraffin tin that William had filled his kettle. The next few moments were like the climax of a nightmare. As he placed the kettle on the spirit stand a sheet of flame burst out, precipitating him through the caravan door and on to the grass outside. Through a whirligig of stars he saw two men who happened to be passing leap into the caravan and fling their coats upon the bright sheet of flame.

The flame died down, to be followed by eddies of smoke. Through the eddies of smoke William, still sitting with blackened face and singed hair upon the grass, saw the scorched remnants of the little girl's dress, now about the size of a pocket handkerchief, still reposing on the chair. Plenty of other things in the caravan had been burnt, but that was all that William's horrified vision could perceive. He gazed at it for a few moments, then the power of movement seemed suddenly to return to him. He sprang to his feet, and fled from the scene of ruin as if he were pursued.

For the next few days he felt as if he were still living in a nightmare. He dare not revisit the little girl; his brain seemed to be numbed and stupefied by the immensity of the catastrophe that had befallen him, and he could think of no means of remedying or mitigating it.

"I *know* he's sickening for something," said Mrs. Brown anxiously to her husband. "He's been so *queer* all the week. When he told Mrs. Monks that he wanted to give his pocket-money to the Sick and Poor Fund, I knew he couldn't be well, and now these last few days he's been so quiet and unlike his usual self."

"Be thankful for small mercies," said Mr. Brown unsympathetically, and went on reading his evening paper.

The day of the garden party arrived. William, with the air of a victim being prepared for sacrifice, allowed himself to be scrubbed and brushed and bundled into his best suit. He made no protests. He was past making protests. He could think of nothing but the little girl deprived by his act of the party to which she had been looking forward. She had said that she would rather go in the old muslin dress than not go at all. And he had burnt the old muslin dress. . . .

He walked slowly and in a hang-dog fashion towards the Hall. The little girl would not be at the party, of course, but suppose she were waiting at the gate to reproach him. . . . The thought made his soul quail in miserable self-abasement. He reached the gates and felt a dull relief when he found that she was not waiting there. He entered the gate and crossed over the lawn to a group of little boys and gaily-dressed little girls. He was picturing a pathetic scene in which he was suddenly attacked by a fatal illness and died here, surrounded by the weeping children.

With his last breath he would send a message to the little girl asking her to forgive him. She would forgive him and weep over his grave. Far better that than that he should go on living with this blot on his honour. His dreams were shattered by a cry of "William", and to his amazement he saw the little girl detach herself from the gaily coloured group and come running across the lawn to him. She wore a very pretty and obviously new dress of pale pink ninon.

"Oh, *William*," she was saying, "you are *wonderful*! Oh, William, thank you so much. It was so clever of you, and I'm so sorry that I didn't really believe you'd got a plan. And it was such a *wonderful* plan."

William was gazing at her, open-mouthed with amazement.

"W-w-w-w-what?" he demanded.

"Why, to burn my old dress so that the insurance people should give me a new one. They've given me a lovely new one, haven't they? Oh, William, it was so clever of you to think of it."

William recovered himself quickly. He assumed his easy swagger, smiling at her in affectionate condescension.

"Oh, that's all right," he said. "A little thing like that's nothin' to me."

Chapter 8

William and the Fisherman

Every June William's father went alone to a country inn for ten days' fishing. William had often begged to be allowed to accompany him, but his requests had always been met by such an uncompromising refusal that he had long since given up all hope. This year, however, to his surprise and delight Fate seemed to be on his side. He had had chicken-pox, and the doctor had decreed that a change of air was necessary before he returned to school.

His mother could not leave her housekeeping duties. The various relatives to whom (though without much real hope) she confided the problem replied kindly and sympathetically, but carefully refrained from inviting William to stay with them.

"You're going away next week, aren't you dear?" said Mrs. Brown to her husband innocently.

He looked at her suspiciously.

"If you mean will I take William," he said firmly, "I most decidedly will not."

But he felt much less firm on the point than he sounded.

If the doctor said that William must have a change of air and he was the only member of the family going away, he didn't see how he could very well refuse to take him with him. He wrote to several relatives who had not yet been approached asking them bluntly if they would care to have William for a few days. They replied as bluntly that they would not.

"Mind you," said Mr. Brown to his wife after having received the last of these replies, "if that boy comes with me, he must look after himself. I'm not going to be responsible for him in any way."

William, on learning that he was to go with his father on the fishing holiday that had been his Mecca from babyhood, could hardly contain his excitement.

He imagined himself accompanying his father and his friends upon all their fishing expeditions. He saw himself making huge catches of trout and salmon before admiring crowds of onlookers. His father seemed to be taking innumerable fishing-rods with him, and William, ever an optimist, thought that he would probably lend him the ones he was not actually using. If his father happened to be using all his rods at once, William then would use his own fishing-rod—a home-made implement consisting of a stick, a piece of string and a bent pin, with which he had distinguished himself at minnow catching in all the local streams. If it would catch minnows, there was, William decided, no reason why it should not catch trout or even salmon. . . . He set off with his father, full of hope, confidence, and excitement.

For the first day he was busy assimilating his impressions. The inn—its *clientèle* consisted entirely of angling enthusiasts—was full of large, purposeful-looking men to whom fishing was real, fishing was earnest; men who treated with silent contempt any remark that did not bear directly and intelligently upon the subject of fishing. At meal-times they sat round a large table in the dining-room in a grim silence broken only by such remarks as: "There was a good hatch of May-fly about quarter-past three," or "They were rising all right, but we couldn't find out what they were taking." Directly after breakfast they would garb themselves in all-enveloping diver-like costumes, collect their tackle and set off, still silent, grim, and purposeful, each to his favourite haunt.

They would not return till the evening and then it was the custom that each should silently and with modest pride lay his catch upon the marble-slabbed hat-stand in the hall of the inn—each catch carefully separate and apart from the others. No one talked of his catch. He merely laid it upon the hat-stand and waited for someone to ask whose it was. News of each catch spread quickly through the community. After dinner again the sportsmen sallied out, solemnly, purposefully, grimly, for the "night rise".

William watched all this with breathless interest. The thought of forming a part of such a community filled him with a fierce and burning pride.

On the first day his father asked him if he would like to come out with him in a boat, and William eagerly agreed. He found the day disappointing. His father landed him on an island in the lake with an empty tobacco box and instructions to catch May-fly in the bushes. William caught three, then became bored and began to experiment with the damming of a small stream and finally to attempt the draining of a miniature bog into which he sank to his knees. When his father returned for him, the three May-flies had escaped and his father, who immediately on reaching the fishing community had yielded to its pervading atmosphere of grim purposefulness, was coldly reproachful. The rest of the day was merely boring. The boatman would not let William try to row. His father would not let him try to fish. He got hopelessly entangled in a spare rod; he

accidentally dropped overboard a box of flies that were
unobtainable locally; he was bitten in the hand by a trout
that he thought was dead, and thereupon gave a yell that
put every other fish for miles around upon its guard.

He disgraced himself completely and finally by standing up to stretch away an attack of pins and needles, and
overbalancing upon his father's rod and breaking it.

"I know one thing," said his father feelingly, "and
that is that you're jolly well not coming out with me in
the boat again."

William was not in any way perturbed by this sentence. It had been a boring and unsatisfactory day and he
was convinced that a day spent by himself on dry land
would be a much more enjoyable affair.

To his surprise and disgust, however, his father
refused to lend him one of his rods. His father, it
appeared, needed all his rods—either for "dapping" or
"trolling" or "casting".

William considered that these people made far too
complicated an affair of the simple exercise of fishing
and set off alone with his home-made rod, a packet of
sandwiches, and a basket lent to him for his "catch" by
the landlady.

He found a suitable stream, fixed a worm on to the
bent pin at the end of his line, and began to fish. His luck
was amazing. He caught minnow after minnow. He
worked hard all morning and all afternoon and returned
in the evening with a laden basket. The other fishermen
had not yet returned. The marble top of the hat-stand
gleamed empty and inviting. William poured the con-
tents of his basket upon it. They covered it completely
with a shining heap of minnows. William gazed at them
with fond pride. Then he got a piece of paper, wrote on
it, "William Brown", and put it on the top of the silvery
heap. That done, glowing with triumph, he awaited the

return of the other fishermen. Not one of them had ever completely filled the marble slab with a single catch like this. He had no doubt at all that he would be the hero of the evening.

Soon he heard the sound of someone approaching and stepped back modestly into the shadow. One of the fishermen—a stalwart young man with a projecting jaw and hooked nose—entered. He looked at the minnow-filled slab, scowled angrily, swept the whole gleaming heap on to the floor with an outraged gesture, rang the bell, said to the housemaid: "Clear up that mess," then with slow deliberate care placed a row of twelve trout on the slab.

William was speechless with indignation at the affront. His first impulse was to hurl himself savagely upon the young man; his second, based upon a consideration of the young man's powerful and muscular frame, was to contain his fury as best he could till an opportunity for a suitable revenge offered itself.

Up to now the fishermen had been identical in William's eyes. They were all large, single-purposed, unsmiling men dressed in enormous waders and devoid of any ideas outside the world of fishing.

Now each detached himself from the mass, as it were, and assumed a distinct personality. There appeared to be two camps of them. The elder ones forgathered in the smoking-room. William's father, who had come to the conclusion many years ago that William was quite capable of looking after himself, and who in any case had from the beginning announced his intention of not allowing him to interfere with his holiday, belonged to the elder camp, and in order to preserve the illusion of a Williamless holiday, had from the first forbidden William to enter the smoking-room. So William, perforce, spent his time with the younger fishermen, and it was therefore the younger fishermen whom he particularly studied.

The leader among them was the muscular youth addressed by his familiars as "Archie" who had swept William's magnificent catch so contemptuously on to the floor. Archie was the most skilful fisherman of the party.

THE FISHERMAN SCOWLED ANGRILY, AND SWEPT THE WHOLE HEAP ON TO THE FLOOR WITH AN OUTRAGED GESTURE.

The others humbly asked his advice and appraised his prowess. Archie's row of trout on the hat-stand slab was always longer than that of any of the others. Archie, moreover, knew the owner of a specially prolific reach of river, and had permission to fish there. He would return from his fishing expedition in this reach laden with spoils and more blatantly pleased with himself each time.

Archie was admired, his advice was sought on all sides, but not even his dearest friends could deny that

WILLIAM WAS SPEECHLESS WITH INDIGNATION.

Archie was overbearing and conceited. It soon became evident that he disliked William as much as William disliked him. The episode of the minnows seemed to him to be a deliberate affront to his dignity, and the presence of William among the party a perpetual outrage. He found fault with William continually, pushing him out of his way whenever he met him, with such lack of ceremony that more than once he sent him sprawling to the ground. He made loud remarks in William's hearing on the unsuitability of having "kids mucking about the place".

"It's never happened before," he said, "and I hope to goodness that it'll never happen again. If it does I shall look out for another place."

William bided his time. He studied his enemy. There was no pretence about Archie's skill as a fisherman. William even followed him secretly down to his private post in the preserved reach and saw him catching trout after trout with an ease and ability that, despite his dislike, William could not help admiring.

He watched him standing in the swirling current in mid-stream up to his waist, still fishing with ease and ability. Certainly in his capacity as fisherman Archie was invulnerable. William tried to find some capacity in which he might be vulnerable, but could find none. For Archie seemed to be nothing but a fisherman. He seemed to have no instincts and desires but those of a fisherman. He seemed to function wholly and entirely upon the fishing plane.

The days passed swiftly by, and William, still enduring Archie's ceaseless snubs, almost began to give up hope of getting his own back. The last week-end of the holiday had arrived, and still Archie had revealed no weakness through which an enemy might avenge himself. His armour seemed to be jointless. Then—two days before

William and his father were to return home—there arrived at the inn an elderly fisherman with his daughter.

The elderly fisherman was negligible enough, but the daughter was not. Even William could see at a glance that this was the sort of girl who made things hum. She had dimples, and dark, curling lashes shading eyes of the deepest blue. Her complexion was smooth and flawless. She had a shatteringly beautiful smile. And William, watching his enemy with ceaseless vigilance, realised at once that Archie was smitten, utterly and uncompromisingly smitten. Smitten, as the saying is, hip and thigh. Only the day before, Archie, after complaining for the thousandth time of having "kids messing about the place," had added: "But thank heaven, at least there aren't any women this year." But now William saw his tanned and healthy countenance deepen to a rich beetroot immediately his eyes fell upon this latest arrival.

The girl, whose name was Claribel, while apparently ignoring the youthful sportsmen and devoting herself entirely to her father, was obviously fully aware of the impression she had made. For not only Archie was smitten, but all the other members of the younger camp were smitten too.

It did not take long for the first shyness to wear off and then began the competition for the damsel's notice. And here Archie's friends, who should have rallied round him, basely deserted him. They did not sing his praises. They did not boost him to the skies as the world's best fisherman. They left him to sing his own praises and boost himself to the skies. To do him justice he was not backward. He boosted himself well and good. He enumerated his recent catches. He described how he alone of all the fishing party could fish with ease when up to his arms in a swirling torrent.

"It's partly a question of balance," he said, "and

partly that I'm—well, I'm a fairly good fisherman, of course."

And Archie stroked his microscopic moustache complacently.

At first Claribel was amused, but gradually she became impressed.

"Come out in the boat with me to-morrow," said Archie, "I'm sure you'll enjoy it. I mean I'm sure you'll find it quite interesting."

Claribel agreed, and William saw yet another triumph in store for the hated Archie. For Claribel, he realised at once, despite her affection of hauteur, belonged to the class of "soppy girls". She swam with the stream and went with the crowd. If fishing were the fashion, then Claribel bags the best fisherman. And without doubt, Archie was the best fisherman. William was very thoughtful that evening.

"Who's the kid?" he heard Claribel ask of Archie.

And Archie replied contemptuously:

"A wretched little oik someone's brought with him."

The next morning was a perfect fishing morning, and Claribel, dressed very fetchingly in pale pink organdie, set off gaily to the river with Archie. He helped her into the boat with a courteous gesture, then the boatman pushed off.

"Isn't this jolly!" William heard Claribel say gaily. "Just like a picnic."

William unobtrusively followed the progress of the boat along the bank, slipping from bush to bush. The strident voice of Archie, enumerating his fishing exploits, reached him clearly across the water.

They reached a point in the river where, only the day before, Archie had stood in mid-stream, the water up to his arm-pits, "casting" with magnificent aplomb, and catching trout after enormous trout. He lowered himself from the boat and took up his stand, a smile of proud anticipation on his lips. He took up his stand and threw his line. Claribel watched him from the boat.

"Now start catching all those fishes you talk about," she said gaily.

Archie had cast his line stylishly enough, but the complacent expression of his face was giving way to uneasiness.

He smiled a ghastly smile at her and said: "Oh, yes . . . you jolly well wait a few minutes. . . ." Then the uneasiness of his expression deepened to panic.

"Hi!" he called suddenly, dropping his rod and clutching wildly at the air. "Hi! Help!"

The boatman hastily brought the boat up to him. He clutched frenziedly at the boatside and then at Claribel. He hung dripping round Claribel's neck. "I'm drowning!" he shouted. "Take me out quick!"

The boat rocked frantically. The boatman and Claribel between them dragged Archie into it. Claribel rendered this assistance involuntarily. Archie, having clasped his arms about her neck in his first spasm of terror, refused to unclasp them, and, long before his large and struggling body was safely landed in the boat, the pale pink organdie was a sodden mass, and Claribel was weeping with fury.

"I couldn't help it," panted Archie. "I t-tell you I was going under. I'd lost my balance. I'd have d-d-drowned if I hadn't caught hold of you. My waders were flooded. I can't t-t-think how. It's a miracle I wasn't drowned. I can't think *how* I wasn't drowned."

"I wish you had been," burst out Claribel passionately. "You've ruined my dress."

"Here's the hole, sir," said the boatman, pointing to an almost imperceptible slit just above the waist of Archie's waders.

"I can't think how it came there," said Archie. "They were all right yesterday." Then to Claribel: "I couldn't help it, I tell you."

"Of *course* you could help it," stormed Claribel. "Making a fool of yourself and me like that! *Deliberately* ruining everything I've got on. I'm soaked, and my dress is *ruined*, I tell you. Take me home at once. I shall never speak to you again as long as I live."

The boatman retrieved the rod, and rowed them back to the landing-place, Archie protesting loudly, Claribel, who had had her say, now gazing over his head with an expression of icy contempt.

William did not come out of cover till they had vanished from view. Then he walked slowly homeward, tenderly fingering the penknife that had punctured Archie's waders and self-esteem.

But William never left anything to chance. He himself had an elder sister of great personal charm, and he had long studied with interest and perpetual surprise the way of a maid with a man. He had learnt that the more angry and unrelenting the maid seems at the actual moment of provocation, the sooner is she likely to relent. So that when he reached the inn he was not surprised to find Claribel and Archie on friendly terms again. Claribel had changed into a blue linen dress that was very becoming, so becoming in fact that she could not help feeling on good terms with herself and the whole world. She was even viewing the episode through a haze of glamour and looking on herself as having rescued Archie from a watery grave. Archie, with more sense than William would have given him credit for, was encouraging this view.

"I simply don't know what I'd have done if you hadn't happened to be there," he was saying.

"Well, of course," said Claribel modestly, "I always

have been considered rather fearless. I mean, I do know how to keep my head in a crisis. I just saw what to do and did it. I'm like that."

"It was wonderful of you," said Archie fervently, "simply *wonderful*. I believe that it's the first morning I've ever come in without catching a single fish. I'll go down to the river this afternoon, however, and see if I can make up for it."

"I expect you will if all I hear of your fishing is true," said Claribel sweetly.

It was very trying for William after all the trouble he had taken to see Archie resuming his old intolerable conceit and Claribel gradually softening towards him. But he had prepared for this, too. Not for nothing had he trudged yesterday into the nearest market town. Moreover, his knowledge of human nature served him well. He was sure that Claribel, after her morning's wetting, would not want to accompany Archie on his afternoon's fishing expedition.

So Archie set off alone. He was away for several hours, and when he returned he proudly laid twelve trout upon the hat-stand, and went to summon Claribel to admire.

He did not see William slip into the hall as he went out of it. When he returned to it with Claribel he saw no difference in the fish that he had laid there. It was Claribel who discovered a wet and illegible fishmonger's ticket adhering to one of them, Claribel whose small but perfect nose discovered the distinctly unpleasant odour of the thirteenth fish—unlucky enough for Archie—that William had deftly introduced into the row. It was in vain that Archie protested and pleaded, in vain that he brought proof incontrovertible that he had actually caught the fish.

Claribel's anger of the afternoon had returned redoubled.

"A nasty, mean, low-down trick to play on me!" she fumed. "A cheat, that's what you are! A nasty, common cheat! Trying to make me think you'd caught them when you'd bought every *one* of them at a fishmonger's—and one of them bad at that! First you try to drown me—yes, and nearly *did* drown me. I could get you put in prison for attempted murder for this morning. I'm sure I could. It was a plot to *murder* me. I don't believe there was a hole in your waders. Or if there was you put it there. And then when you've not been able to murder me you try to make a fool of me by pretending to have caught fish when you've been out to buy them. I hate you, and I'll never speak to you again as long as I live. I always thought fishermen were cheats and liars, and now I know they are. *And* murderers. I hate all of you. I shan't stay a minute longer in the beastly place."

Leaving Archie opening and shutting his mouth silently like one of his own expiring fish, she swept into the smoking-room, where her father sat swopping fishing yarns with some members of the elder camp. He was surprised but in no way discomposed by his daughter's sudden decision to go home. He had long ago accustomed himself to sudden changes of plans on the part of his female belongings. Moreover, he knew that she had only accompanied him on an impulse, leaving behind her several interesting "affairs" from which a good deal of kick could still be extracted. He had had a suspicion that the place would fail to supply the excitement that was necessary to a girl of Claribel's temperament, and on the whole was not sorry to hear her decision.

"All right, my dear," he said mildly, "but I'm afraid you can't leave this minute, because there isn't a train till to-morrow afternoon."

She did not come downstairs that evening. She spent it packing in her bedroom, while Archie hung about the hall, still opening and shutting his mouth silently, as if practising passionate speeches of protestation.

The next morning after breakfast Claribel directed the shattering smile at William and said: "Will you come for a walk with me this morning, William?"

William accepted the invitation with apparent eagerness, though he remained completely unshattered by the smile. He knew that Claribel had fixed on the "wretched little oik" with a true womanly intuition of what would be most galling to Archie. They spent the whole morning together. William found it intolerably boring. Claribel was the most limited human being whom he had ever met. She was wholly ignorant on the subject of pirates or smugglers or Red Indians. She was not interested in climbing trees, or damming streams, or getting through barbed-wire fences, or exploring the countryside. She was frightened of spiders, and she did not know a toad from a frog. Relations became definitely strained between them as the morning wore on, and Claribel grew more and more irritable, especially when William took her a short cut back to the inn that led directly through a bog. William persisted that the bog was now all right, as he had drained it three days before, but Claribel's dainty shoes bore ample evidence that this statement of William's erred on the side of optimism. Her resentment against the wretched Archie, however, still blazed so brightly that as soon as they came within sight of the inn she turned her shattering smile on to William again and began to talk to him with every appearance of affectionate interest.

The sight of Archie lurking morosely in the hall when they entered assured her that her efforts were not being wasted.

"WILL YOU COME FOR A WALK WITH ME THIS MORNING, WILLIAM?" CLARIBEL ASKED.

During lunch she continued to talk brightly to William. After lunch the station bus drew up at the front door, and Claribel, attired for the journey, stepped into it. Archie sprang forward desperately.

"Listen!" he said. "Just listen! Just let me explain!"

But Claribel turned to William with the shattering smile and said:

"Good-bye, William darling, and thank you so much for being so sweet to me."

Then the bus swept her away, still waving effusively to William. Archie gave a hollow laugh, and William slipped away before Archie should try to find outlet for his feelings.

William and his father were going home the next day, so it was not difficult for William to avoid Archie's vengeance in the interval.

Failing to find William, Archie wreaked his vengeance on the fishes and brought in a phenomenal catch that he flung carelessly upon the slab, repeating the hollow laugh.

"Did you enjoy it, William dear?" asked William's mother when he reached home.

William considered the question in silence for a moment, then said:

"Yes, on the whole, I did—quite . . . especially the end part."

Chapter 9

William and the Drug Trafficker

Robert was, of course, indirectly responsible for the whole thing. William had been kept indoors with a cold for a week, and Robert had good-naturedly lent him a few of the volumes with which be beguiled his less highbrow moments. Most of them dealt with the murderers and amateur detectives who were now almost as familiar to William as his own beloved pirates and Red Indians. But one of them opened up entirely new ground. It was concerned with the drug traffic, and in the book the traffic was carried on by people of apparently the highest respectability. Elderly maiden ladies of impeccable appearance handed small twists of paper to simple old men whose interests seemed to centre entirely in their gardens. Clergymen with long, white beards threw minute packages from carriage windows as trains flashed by stations, and these were picked up as if quite casually by earnest-looking men wearing the Salvation Army uniform.

The seeming respectability—even holiness—of every member of the gang made the work of the hero, who was engaged in tracking them, extremely difficult.

William found the book so engrossing that he read it far into the night, propping up a rug against his bedroom door so that his mother would not see the line of light beneath it when she came to bed. The next morning he looked on the world around him with changed eyes. So powerful an impression had the book made on him that even the sight of his mother handing a ten-shilling note to the baker's man roused in him feelings of the deepest suspicion. He began to haunt the Vicar, the doctor, the superintendent of the Sunday School, and the many elderly ladies of impeccable appearance who lived in the neighbourhood. His hopes at first were very high, but as the days passed and he failed to find any actual proof of guilt, he grew tired of shadowing them, and would have forgotten the affair entirely had it not been for the arrival of a college friend of Robert's who had been invited to spend part of the vacation at the Browns'. He was nineteen, the same age as Robert, and of such a particularly guileless appearance—mild blue eyes, lank hair, and a high-pitched voice—that William's interest and suspicions sprang at once to life again. The guest was, moreover, of a studious turn of mind, and insisted on Robert's reading with him for an imminent exam during the greater part of the morning.

William was convinced that this wholly unnatural display of zeal marked some nefarious plot. He shadowed him continually, carefully examining the soles of his shoes, the back of his clothes-brush, his mattress, and various other places suitable for the concealment of drugs. The friend—his name, Rupert Bergson, was in itself almost a proof of guilt—obeyed the convention by which small brothers of eleven are as completely ignored as if they did not exist, and, following Robert's example, never acknowledged William's presence by word or look. This attitude was to William a further proof—if further proof were needed—that Rupert Bergson was engaged in some criminal pursuit. His ignoring of William proved a guilty conscience. He was afraid of giving himself away.

One morning Rupert set off for a walk alone, leaving Robert reading in his bedroom. William shadowed him with his usual elaborate air of secrecy, his coat collar turned up, his cap well over his eyes.

Instead of going for one of the walks that he and Robert usually took, Rupert followed the short cut to the station through the fields and churchyard. William enjoyed shadowing him through the churchyard, dodging from tombstone to tombstone. It was a proceeding that appealed strongly to his sense of the dramatic. When the guest reached the station William at first thought that he had realised his suspicions and decided on flight.

Crouching behind the only luggage truck William eagerly awaited events. Rupert Bergson stood upon the platform, his hands in his pockets, unaware of the stern gaze that William bent on him from behind his luggage truck. Suddenly a train came through the station. It did not stop, but as it passed a youth who was leaning out of a carriage window threw a piece of paper folded into the shape of a cocked hat at Rupert's feet. Rupert picked it up, put it in his pocket, then set off briskly homewards. So impressed was William by this confirmation of his darkest suspicions that he remained absent-mindedly crouching behind his truck till the porter—an old enemy—rudely interrupted his reverie, seized him by the collar and ejected him ungently from the premises.

William picked himself up, gave a short, harsh laugh, which was meant to express dark hints of vengeance on the porter, then ran off quickly after his quarry, catching him up just as he reached the Browns' house. He followed him into the hall and up the stairs. Rupert opened the door of Robert's bedroom and entered. Before the door was shut William heard Robert say:

AS THE TRAIN PASSED A YOUTH THREW A PIECE OF PAPER
FOLDED INTO THE SHAPE OF A COCKED HAT AT RUPERT'S FEET.

"Got it?" and heard Rupert's reply: "Yes . . . he threw
it out from the train."

William went slowly and thoughtfully downstairs. So
Robert was in it, too. That rather complicated matters.
He could not simply inform the police of the matter if
Robert was in it, too. He could not very well hand over
his only brother to certain penal servitude. . . . He must
go very carefully. The situation called for finesse and
resource.

All that afternoon the two remained in Robert's bedroom with the door shut, and William, hovering about outside, imagined them lying on luxurious divans (Robert's room did not contain any luxurious divans, but in his book drug takers and luxurious divans were so inextricably connected that William could not imagine one without the other) smoking pipes of opium and inhaling cocaine. They emerged at tea-time looking tired and wan, and William shook his head sorrowfully over their plight. He decided to appeal to Robert's better self and, approaching him when he was alone in the morning-room, said earnestly:

"Robert, I'd give it up if I was you. I'd give it up altogether."

It happened that Mrs. Brown had just been suggesting to Robert that he smoked too much, and Robert, thinking that William had overheard the conversation, turned on him indignantly.

"Well, I'm not going to, so you can shut up and mind your own business."

So ferocious did Robert sound that William decided to cease his appeal to his better self and took himself off as quickly as possible, shaking his head sadly over the effects of opium and cocaine upon the temper.

He made up his mind to find some means of handing Rupert Bergson over to justice without involving Robert, but it was several days before the opportunity presented itself.

It happened that the whole family, including the maids, was going to a display of local talent in the Village Hall, and that at the last moment Rupert Bergson, who had suddenly developed a cold in his head, said that he could not go with them.

"It's dod kide to go addywhere wid a code like dis," he said. "I'd rather stay at hobe."

"All right," agreed Robert, "and if you want anything to do you might clear out that old cupboard in my room—the one where my old cups and things are."

No sooner had the family taken its seats in the Village Hall than William, very quietly and unobtrusively, slipped from his chair and set off homeward again. In any case he was not interested in local talent. No one noticed that he had gone.

He opened the front door of his home and, creeping up the stairs, peeped cautiously through the half-open door of Robert's bedroom.

There upon the floor knelt Rupert Bergson, conscientiously engaged in clearing out the cupboard. Around him on the floor stood various cups that had been won by Robert in his schooldays and, after being kept on the dining-room sideboard for several years, had been relegated to Robert's bedroom cupboard owing to complaints from the domestic staff about the time they took to clean.

William crept downstairs again and out into the road. His next step was to find the policeman but, as generally happens on such occasions, the policeman was not to be found. At last, however, William found him standing outside the Blue Lion lost in gloomy contemplation of his own boots.

"I say! Come quick!" said William. "There's a burglar in our house!"

The policeman turned startled eyes upon him.

"A what?" he said.

"A burglar," said William. "We'd all gone to the thing at the Village Hall, and I came home because—because I'd forgotten my handkerchief, and I found a burglar in Robert's bedroom."

"Where?" said the policeman. He spoke eagerly, and his whole aspect brightened. His life since joining the police a year ago had been one long and bitter disillusionment. He had not even been able to catch a motorist with his tail light out.

"Where?" he repeated. "Take me there quickly."

William took him to the house, led him up the stairs, and flung open the door of Robert's bedroom.

Rupert Bergson sat on the floor in front of the open cupboard surrounded by Robert's cups.

"That's him," said William.

RUPERT SAT IN FRONT OF THE CUPBOARD, SURROUNDED BY
ROBERT'S CUPS. "THAT'S HIM," SAID WILLIAM.

"Now then, what are you doing with those cups?"
said the policeman sternly to Rupert Bergson.

Rupert Bergson looked at him in surprise.

"I'b tidyig the cupboard," he explained.

"That's a nice tale!" said the policeman scornfully.
"What are you doing in this house at all?"

"I'b stayig here," said Rupert Bergson. "I'b stayig in
the house."

The policeman turned to William.

"He isn't," said William firmly.

"I'b stayig with his brother," said Rupert
indignantly. "I'b his brother's friend. I'b been here for
over a week."

William met his gaze unblinkingly.

"No, he isn't," he said. "I've never seen him
before."

"You see it's no use making up tales like that," said
the policeman sternly to Rupert Bergson. "You'd better
come quietly."

William's plan was working out more successfully
than he had dared to hope. He had thought that if he
could get Rupert arrested for burglary with evidences of
his drug trafficking guilt upon him (and he was sure to
have evidences of his drug trafficking guilt upon him) he
would be delivered over to justice without Robert's
coming into it at all.

"And he's a drug trafficker, too," went on William
excitedly. "You look in his pockets and I bet you find
some."

Rupert Bergson's utter bewilderment gave him all the
appearance of guilt. The policeman plunged his hand
into his coat pocket and brought out the paper folded
into the shape of a cocked hat that William had seen
thrown upon the station platform.

"That's it," shouted William triumphantly. "Open it.

You'll find cocaine in it."

"Id's an oudrage," said Rupert Bergson furiously.

The policeman had opened the paper and was slowly reading out the words that were written on it:

"Translate II. 260–360 and comment on the following constructions, giving parallel examples where possible."

At that moment there came the sound of footsteps and voices from the hall. The Browns were returning from the entertainment. Local talent, though well meaning, was limited, and William had taken a long time to find the policeman. They came upstairs and stood in an amazed group at Robert's door, gazing at William, the policeman, and the distraught Rupert Bergson. The policeman was still studying the note with a puzzled expression.

"What on earth's all this?" said Mr. Brown.

"Good Lord!" said Robert looking at the paper in the policeman's hand. "Why, it's the test paper."

"What test paper?" said Mrs. Brown weakly.

"Bergson's cousin was with some men at a reading party, and they'd got their tutor to set them a test paper to do at the end, and we thought we'd like to try our hand at it, too, as we've been doing the same book, so we asked Bergson's cousin to let us have it, and as his train went through the station here he said he'd chuck it out as he passed—less trouble than posting it. So he did, and we worked through it that afternoon. But what on earth—?"

"An oudrage, I dell you," repeated Rupert Bergson fiercely.

The policeman was beginning to look as mystified as the rest of them.

"Well, this boy—" he began.

Then he turned round to look for William.

But William was nowhere to be seen.

William was in fact already little more than a dot on the distant horizon.

Chapter 10

April Fool's Day

April the First was a day generally enjoyed to the full by William, but this year something seemed to have gone wrong. Not one of his efforts had been successful. Ethel had calmly put on one side, without even attempting to crack it, the empty egg-shell that he had carefully arranged in her egg-cup; Robert had removed the upturned tintack from his chair before sitting down, and had placed it so neatly upon William's that William had been taken unawares; his father had refused even to raise his eyes from his newspaper at William's excited: "Look, father, there's a cow in the garden"; and his mother had merely murmured: "Yes, dear," when William had informed her that Ethel had been bitten by a mad dog on her way to the village.

His attempts to make April Fools of his Outlaws had been no more successful. They were all, indeed, so much upon their guard that none of them would answer the simplest question or pay heed to the most innocent remark. At last they abandoned hostilities and formed an offensive alliance against the other boys of the neighbourhood. But not even this was successful. The other boys of the neighbourhood, also, were too well up in the rules of the game to be taken in by the well-worn tricks the Outlaws played on them. Advised of the near approach of bulls, runaway horses, motor-cars out of control, they merely made long noses at the Outlaws. Informed that sweets were being given away at the local sweet shop, that a circus had just arrived at the other end of the village, that Farmer Jenks was riding round his farmyard on his old sow, they merely remarked: "Yah! April Fools yourself!"

"I wish we could find someone that had forgotten it was April Fool's Day," said Henry.

"Tell you what I'd like to do," said William dreamily. "I'd like to make someone really important, like the King or Parliament, an April Fool."

"You couldn't."

"Yes, I could. I could eas'ly. I could ring them up and say that an enemy had landed and they'd call out the army and march down to the coast and find no one there. I bet they'd be April Fools all right."

"You don't know their telephone number."

"No, but I could look them up in the book, couldn't I, silly?"

"You'd prob'ly get executed."

"Yes, I know. That's why I'm not goin' to do it. Not to the King and Parliament anyway. But I'd like to make someone important an April Fool, but not as important as the King or Parliament. Let's think who's the most important person living here."

"The Vicar," suggested Ginger.

"The doctor," suggested Douglas.

"Yes, I think the doctor," said William. "He'd be easier to make one, anyway . . . I know! I've thought of something to bring them *both* in."

Followed by his Outlaws, William made his way up to the doctor's front door, knocked at it smartly, and informed the maid who opened it that the Vicar was dying and would the doctor please go to him at once. For answer he received a box on the ear that nearly made him lose his balance. He rejoined his friends, rubbing his boxed ear tenderly and filled with righteous indignation.

"S'pose it was true, an' they'd let the poor Vicar die. Well, I think she's the same as a murderer, that woman is. I've a good mind to go an' *tell* the Vicar that she's as good as murdered him. I bet I was as near dead as you could be, too, with a bang like that on the side of my head. She ought to get put in prison for murdering both of us. I'm jolly well sick of April Fool's Day, anyway. I vote we go and play somewhere. . . ."

It was decided that it would be hardly safe to play in their own village. Their own village was too full of their enemies, eager to use the noble festival of All Fool's Day as an opportunity of getting even with them. They could not safely relax their guard for a moment in their own village.

"Let's go to Marleigh," suggested Ginger, "an' take the football with us."

Marleigh was a village about two miles away. The Outlaws were comparatively unknown at Marleigh.

"Good!" agreed William. "We'll get a bit of peace there."

They set off briskly across the fields to Marleigh, and there found a vacant plot of land on which to hold a football match. The Outlaws considered four the ideal number for a football match.

"A beastly house next to it, of course," said William morosely (William was still smarting in body and spirit from his treatment at the hands of the doctor's house-maid), "and they'll be sure to make a beastly fuss every time the ball goes into the garden. I don't think there's a single place left to play in in England that hasn't got a house next to it, all ready to make a fuss the minute your ball goes into its garden. Sometimes I feel I don't care how soon the end of the world comes."

"Well, come on, let's begin to play," said Ginger, anxious to wean William from his mood of melancholy.

They began to play, and in a few minutes, as William had prophesied, their ball went over the wall into the garden of the next house. It was a high brick wall with no convenient foothold on it, so they went to the gate to survey the enemy's ground. There they found that to get round to the side garden where their ball was, they would have to pass a window where a haughty-looking lady sat at a writing-table. Clearly it could not be done.

"We'll have to go to the door and ask," said William cheerfully. (William's spirits always rose at a crisis.) "I'll put on my polite look. Am I clean an' tidy?"

William was far from being clean and tidy, but the Outlaws had not very high standards in those matters.

"You're all right," said Ginger. "Go on. Put on your polite look."

William's polite look, though much admired by himself and his friends, was in reality a sickly leer. It certainly did not seem to ingratiate him with the house-maid who opened the door.

"Please can we go round to your garden to get our ball, if you don't mind, thank you very much?"

The housemaid stared at him disapprovingly, disappeared, and soon returned to say shortly:

"She says it's an intolerable nuisance, but you can this once."

"Thank you very much," said William, widening his leer and making her a courtly bow.

"None of your impudence!" she said, and slammed the door in his face.

The Outlaws went round to the side of the house and found the ball.

"Cranky old thing, wasn't she?" said Ginger.

"I don't think she was bad," said William judicially.

"THANK YOU VERY MUCH," SAID WILLIAM, MAKING A COURTLY BOW.

"She didn't murder me anyway, same as the other one did."

They returned to the plot of waste land and continued their interrupted match. In five minutes the ball had gone over the wall again. They considered the situation with some dismay.

"I'm not going to ask again," said William firmly. "She'll start murdering me same as the other one did if I go. You'd better go, Ginger."

"All right," said Ginger, and began to compose his features into an imitation of William's leer as he walked up to the front door.

The same housemaid opened it, received Ginger's dulcet request with obvious indignation, then retired to report it to her mistress. She returned almost immediately.

"She says you ought to be ashamed of yourselves pestering like this. She says you can get it this once, but she says she'll send for the police if it goes on."

"Gosh!" said Ginger, rejoining his friends. "More like dragons than yuman bein's round here, aren't they? We'll take jolly good care not to let it go over again, anyway."

They returned to their game of football, but in five minutes an energetic and unguarded kick from Douglas had sent the ball once more into the forbidden garden.

"Well, it's you or Henry to get it now," said William, "me an' Ginger's had our turns."

"Yes an' get put in prison," said Douglas indignantly. "You'd like me to get put in prison, wouldn't you, all chained up and only bread an' water to eat?"

"I shouldn't mind," said William, unmoved by this harrowing picture. "I shouldn't mind a bit. It's all your fault kickin' it over after what she said."

"They all look pretty savage about here," said Ginger. "They look as if they'd kill you as soon as look at you. I votes we go home an' leave it."

"Yes, I dare say you do," said William. "It's not your football. It's my football, an' I'm not goin' home without it, so there!"

"What are you goin' to do then?"

"I'm goin' to get it. I'm goin' to crawl round to the garden on my hands and knees, so's she can't see me from the window, an' get it."

"I'll come with you," said Ginger.

"So will I," said Douglas and Henry.

There was no need for more than one to go to fetch the ball, but when there was any danger the Outlaws liked to face it together. In single file, on hands and knees, they made their way to the garden and retrieved the ball. In single file, on hands and knees, they began their journey back. But, just as they were passing beneath the window, Ginger sneezed, and the amazed and indignant face of the lady of the house appeared at the window, disappeared, then reappeared, now more indignant than amazed, at the front door. The Outlaws rose sheepishly to their feet. The lady stood barring their path and giving eloquent voice to her indignation.

"Disgraceful! . . . *disgraceful!* I've a good mind to send for the police and give you in charge for trespassing. If I ever see any of you inside this garden again, I'll send for the police at *once*. . . . Go away this *minute*. If I knew who your parents were I'd write to them most strongly."

The Outlaws fled precipitately, William clutching his beloved ball.

"Crumbs!" he said, "I was afraid she'd take it from me. She looks as if she'd steal as well as murder, soon as look at anyone. Crumbs, wasn't she awful? That's twice to-day I've jus' escaped bein' murdered."

"I votes we don't play here any more," said Ginger.

"No, I votes we don't," said William, "not with my ball, anyway. P'raps it's time to go home, anyway."

"Yes, it's nearly twelve," said Ginger, pretending to consult his watch (which never went for more than five

"I'VE A GOOD MIND TO SEND FOR THE POLICE AND GIVE YOU IN
CHARGE," SHE SAID.

minutes) but in reality glancing at the church clock that
showed above the trees.

"Nearly twelve," said William wistfully, "and we've
not made anyone an April Fool. It'll be the first year I
ever remember that we've not made anyone an April
Fool."

"We've not been made one ourselves, anyway,"

Ginger reminded him.

"'Course not!" said William scornfully. "Catch anyone makin' April Fools of us! That's not the point. The point is that we've not made anyone one. It seems awful somehow not to have made anyone an April Fool on April Fool's Day."

"Well, it's not quite twelve yet," said Ginger; "it's not too late."

"Yes, but who is there to make one here?" said William.

At that moment a boy was seen coming towards them. He was fat and pale, and he looked both stupid and conceited. The Outlaws took an immediate dislike to him.

"Let's make *him* one," whispered William.

"Yes, but *how*?" said Ginger.

William frowned, then his frown cleared into a beatific smile.

"I know!" he said.

The boy had come abreast of them now. He gave them a challenging grimace.

"I say," said William with well-assumed friendliness, "what do you like best? What sort of cakes, I mean?"

"Coconut buns," answered the boy promptly.

William gave a short, surprised laugh.

"Well, that's a funny thing." He pointed to the house that had been the scene of their escapade. "You see that house?"

"Yes," said the boy.

"Well, the lady that lives there, she always gives coconut buns to any boys who come to ask if they can get their ball from her garden. If you want some coconut buns all you have to do is to go up to the door and knock and ask if you can speak to the mistress of the house. And when you get to her all you've got to say is that you're one of the boys who've been playing ball just outside her garden this morning, and the ball's gone over again and may you fetch it. And when you've said that she'll give you some coconut buns."

The boy stared at them.

"Go on," William urged him, glancing at the clock and seeing the fingers perilously near the fatal hour. "Go on. We *want* you to have those buns 'cause—'cause you look hungry. See here"—desperately he took a treasured whistle from his pocket—"I'll give you that if you'll go an' say it."

The boy took and pocketed it without a word.

William's urgency had communicated itself to the others. They felt that their very honour depended upon somehow or other making this boy an April Fool before twelve o'clock.

"And look here," said Ginger feverishly. "I'll give you this penknife, too, if you'll go quick. We—we *want* you to have those coconut buns."

The boy pocketed the penknife, too, stared at them for another moment, then said: "A'right," and, walking up to the front door, rang the bell. The housemaid opened it and he was admitted. The door closed. The Outlaws danced a silent dance of triumph and delight at the gate. Then they waited impatiently for the fleeing form of their victim to issue, pursued by the wrath of the redoubtable lady of the house. Nothing happened.

"Perhaps she's rung up the police," said William, looking anxiously down the road for the form of a policeman.

"Well, if she has, we've made April Fools of all of them," said Ginger triumphantly.

"I—I hope she's not murderin' him," said Douglas. "We shall get into a beastly row if we've got him murdered."

But at that moment an upstairs window was flung open, and the boy appeared at it. He held a coconut bun in one hand, the whistle and penknife in the other. He grinned and munched and waved his spoils at them exultantly.

"W-w-w-what are you doing there?" stammered William.

"I live here," shouted the boy. "It's my home. Yah-boo! April Fools!"

He laid down the coconut bun and took up a pea-shooter.

The clock from the church tower struck twelve.

"April Fools!" called the boy again.

The Outlaws turned and began to walk slowly down the road.

A pea caught William neatly just above one ear.

Chapter 11

William Makes Things Hum

As William passed down the road a casual observer would merely have seen a rather dirty small boy, stockings coming down, collar bearing the impression of his own grubby fingers, cap placed awry on a shock of untidy hair, swaggering along and brandishing a stick that had obviously once formed part of the hedgerows. But William himself saw quite a different picture. He saw a tall, sinister figure, patch over one eye, coloured handkerchief round waist, brandishing a naked sword in his hands. The country lane behind him was not empty, but filled with the gallant band of buccaneers who were his followers. He had just made a shipload of his enemies walk the plank. He was now on his way to attack the stronghold of a rival company of pirates. He stopped, took a bottle from his pocket and raised it to his lips with a flourish. It was really liquorice water, but to William it was smuggled rum of a rare and potent brand. Then he pocketed it and marched along again, with so large a swagger that, turning a bend in the road, he ran full tilt into a boy who was coming from the opposite direction. He was a bigger boy than William, and even more gloriously dirty and untidy, with a shock of bright red hair. William felt an instinctive respect for him and a desire to impress him.

"Think the world belongs to you, don't you?" said the boy, recovering first from the impact.

"Huh!" said William, "it jolly nearly does anyway. I've jus' made three hundred people walk the plank, an' when I've finished conquering the pirates I'm after now, I'll be the biggest pirate chief in the world, and I bet I conquer the whole world. I've got the biggest army in the world already."

He waved his hand with an airy swagger at the empty lane behind him.

The other boy laughed.

"That's story-book stuff!" he said. "Well, would you like to known what *I've* done this afternoon?"

"Yes," said William, "I would."

"Well, first I drove all the ducks from Farmer Brewster's pond to Farmer Jenks's pond, so there'll be a nice old mess-up when they find out. Then I drove all the sheep out of his field into the lane, and I 'spect they'll be at Timbuctoo by now. Then I let his cows into the turnip stack. Then I collected all the eggs from the poultry-house and put them under the broody hen in the hedge. Then I filled my pockets from his apple loft, and now I'm going home."

"Golly!" said William, deeply impressed.

"You see, he'd annoyed me," explained the boy simply; "and when people annoy me—well, there's always something coming to them. The ole foreman chased me, but it takes more than any ole foreman to catch me."

He laughed again, and walked on down the road with a swagger that put even William's swagger to shame. William stared after him open-mouthed. His own imaginary adventures had faded into utter insignificance in the face of this convincing recital. The pirate exploits were, after all, completely impossible, but this. . . .

Suddenly he decided to adopt the red-headed boy's adventures as his own. He wasn't a pirate chief any longer. He was the boy who had driven Farmer Brewster's ducks into Farmer Jenks's pond, let out the sheep and cows, hidden his day's supply of eggs under a broody hen, and robbed his apple loft. And all because Farmer Brewster had annoyed him. He laughed—a laugh that was a faithful copy of the red-headed boy's laugh.

"When people annoy me," he said darkly, "well, there's always something coming to them."

He went on his way down the road with a new swagger, a swagger more rollicking and daredevil than his old one—the red-headed boy's swagger.

At the next bend in the lane he met a little girl. Her dark hair was cropped short, and her face was round and dimpled. She stopped and looked at him with an interest that William found irresistible. After all, what was the use of having so thrilling a story to tell if there was no one to tell it to?

"Hello," said the little girl.

"Hello," responded William, and added with the newly acquired daredevil laugh: "Would you like to know what *I've* been doing this afternoon?"

"Yes, I would," said the little girl, and turned obligingly to walk along the road with him.

William intensified his new swagger.

"Well," he said, "I drove the ducks from Farmer Brewster's pond to Farmer Jenks's pond, so there'll be a nice old mess-up when they find out. Then I drove his sheep out of their field up the lane, and they'll be at Timbuctoo by now, I expect. And then I let his cows into the turnip stack and put all his eggs under a broody hen and filled my pockets from his apple loft. His foreman ran after me, but it takes more than an ole foreman to catch me. You see," explained William, repeating the daredevil laugh, "he'd annoyed me, and when people annoy me there's always something coming to them."

Yes, the story was much more artistically satisfying than his pirate story. He enjoyed the recital immensely. He was just going to improve upon it still further and had begun: "And then after that—" when he noticed a large man in gaiters coming through a gate into the lane.

"Uncle!" called the little girl excitedly. "This is the boy—the boy what mixed up your ducks and let out the sheep and cows and took the eggs and apples. He's just told me he's the boy. . . ."

An iron grip descended upon William's neck.

"So *you're* the boy, are you?" said a voice that sent cold shivers up and down William's spine. "Well, then, you're the boy I've been looking for all morning. Come along with me."

William felt himself impelled along the road by the iron grip.

"No, please, I'm not the boy," he protested breathlessly; "I was only pretendin'. Honest, I was only pretendin'. It was another boy what did it an' he told me he'd done it an' I was pretendin' I'd done it an'—"

"Talking won't do you any good," said the ruthless voice, "so you may as well shut up."

William struggled desperately against the iron grip, but in vain. He was dragged ignominiously along the road, pitifully bereft of his swagger. Between his ineffectual struggles to escape he continued his explanation.

"You see—it was—this other—boy what did it—he told—me he'd—done it an' so—I pretended—it was me what—did it, just for fun. Please—I didn't—really do it— Please, I didn't really—"

"If I wanted to make up a tale," said the grim voice scornfully, "I'd try to make up a better one than that. Shut up and come along."

AN IRON GRIP DESCENDED ON WILLIAM'S NECK. "SO YOU'RE
THE BOY, ARE YOU?" SAID A VOICE.

The grip of iron tightened till it almost choked him,
and he was dragged through a gate into a farmyard and
towards a shed.

"I tell you what I'm going to do with you," said the
grim voice. "I'm going to shut you in this shed, and then
I'm going to fetch a policeman, and we'll see what the

magistrates have to say about your pranks."

He pushed William into the shed, turned the key, and departed.

William looked around him. There was only one small window, with a broken pane, too high up for him to reach.

He struggled with the door for some time, but it was securely bolted on the outside. Suddenly he saw the little girl at the window.

"Hello," she said, "I've climbed up a tree to have a look at you. He's gone to fetch a policeman."

"I know," said William, trying without much success to assume a nonchalant air.

"I expect you'll get put in prison."

William attempted the daredevil laugh, but it was so complete a failure that he turned it into a cough.

"I expect you'll get put in prison for years an' *years*," went on the little girl.

"I'll give you all the money I've got if you'll let me out," said William.

"How much money have you got?" said the little girl with interest.

William examined his pockets.

"I've got a halfpenny here, an' I've got threepence in my money-box. I *think* I've threepence in it. *Nearly* threepence, anyway. An' I'm goin' to start having pocket-money again when they've paid for the new landing window. That'll be threepence a week. I'll give you all my pocket-money for weeks an' *weeks* when they start givin' it me again if you'll let me out."

"You won't be able to have pocket-money in prison," said the little girl. "An' you'll only have bread an' water to eat," she went on, seeming to take a gloomy relish in the situation; "an' I expect you'll be there for years and *years*. They always send people to prison for years and *years*. Prob'ly for the rest of your life."

"You don't know anything about it," said William, but he did not sound much more confident than he felt.

"I do," persisted the little girl. "I know a *lot* about it. I once read a book about a man who was in prison for years and *years*. And then, in the end, his wife went in and changed clothes with him, and he got away in her clothes and she stayed in prison in his, but they let her out when they found it wasn't him."

"If you'll unbolt the door," said William, "I'll give you all my cigarette cards."

He had decided some time ago that cigarette card collecting was unworthy of a pirate chief.

"How many have you got?"

"A hundred."

"Oo!" said the little girl. "A *hundred*?"

"Yes."

"Will you give them me *all*?"

"Yes."

"Well"—she considered the situation, and her excitement died away—"it isn't any use, anyway, because uncle told Mr. Greg—the foreman—to keep an eye on the shed and see you didn't get away before he came back with the policeman. *Tell* you what," she went on in sudden excitement, "let's change clothes like the people did in that tale I read. That's a *jolly* good idea. I'll put on your suit and pretend I'm a boy. I've always wanted to be a boy. Then you can go out, and they'll think it's me."

William looked at her doubtfully.

"You're a good bit smaller than what I am," he said. "I don't think anyone'd think I was you."

But the little girl eagerly defended her project.

"Oh, yes, they would. I'll take off my frock and throw it down to you through the window an' I'll throw down a long stick an' you can give me your suit up on the end of it. I think it's a *lovely* idea. *Just* like the people in the book. Take off your suit, and I'll take off my frock. Then I'll come back and give you my frock, and you can give me your suit."

A few moments later a small, pink cotton frock fluttered down through the window, followed by a long stick. William took the bottle of liquorice water from his pocket, drained it lovingly, then handed up his suit on the end of the stick to the little girl, and began to struggle into the pink cotton frock.

Soon the little girl was again at the window, clad in William's well-worn tweed suit. It was far too big for her, but her face beamed with satisfaction.

"Isn't it *lovely*," she said. "Now I can pretend I'm a boy. I've always wanted to be a boy."

William, who felt that somehow his rescue was being lost sight of in her excitement over the possession of his suit, was less enthusiastic.

"It won't meet anywhere," he said still struggling with the pink cotton frock. "No one would think I was you. I can't escape in this thing. It's a rotten idea. Give me back my own suit."

But the little girl still seemed to have forgotten that the object of the change of costume was the rescue of William.

"No," she said firmly, "I *like* your suit. I'm going to keep it. It's much nicer to climb trees in than an old girl's dress."

She vanished from the window.

"Hi!" called William desperately. "Come back. Give me my suit."

But there was no answer, and the voice of the little girl, singing joyfully to herself, died away in the distance. William realised that he was in a worse plight than ever. The pink cotton dress was so ludicrously small for him that it would not only make escape impossible but would considerably detract from his dignity during his progress from the farm to prison. If he had to go to prison for the rest of his life, at least he would like his journey thither to be accomplished as impressively as possible.

But the little girl had not quite forgotten him, after all. She appeared again suddenly at the window, and began to stuff through the hole in the pane, first a large, dark shawl, then a battered bonnet, rakishly trimmed with faded artificial violets.

"*Those'll* cover you all right," she said. "They're Mrs. Hobbin's, the charwoman's. Put on the bonnet an' tie it under your chin an' then put the shawl right round you an' I'll open the door for you an' Mr. Greg'll think you're Mrs. Hobbin going home because you've come over funny. She often goes home because she's come over funny."

William gratefully decided to give the little girl his old whistle as well as his collection of cigarette cards. He had long meant to give away the old whistle when he found some worthy recipient. Though it whistled no longer, it was large and important-looking.

The bonnet came well down over his head, and the shawl enveloped him from neck to feet. No sooner had he thus arrayed himself, than he heard the sound of the latch being gently withdrawn, and the little girl peeped in.

"Come along," she whispered. "Mr. Greg's just gone to put the milk cans out, but he'll come back any minute. . . ."

William gathered up his shawl and fled across the farmyard and down the road. Finding that he was not pursued and realising that his haste was inconsistent with his disguise, he slackened his pace and began to walk along with an odd, lurching gait intended to combine the appearance of old age with as much speed as possible. As he went he looked anxiously about for his own suit. He soon saw it following him and stopped a minute for it to overtake him.

"Wasn't that clever of me?" said its wearer complacently.

"Let's get somewhere quick where we can change," said William; "I want to get back into my own things. I keep tumbling over the shawl and this beastly hat tickles my face."

"But I *like* wearing your suit," said the little girl firmly, "an', anyway, you're supposed to be disguised. The man in the story kept on his wife's things till he'd got into another country. You ought to go to another country."

"Well, I'm not going to," said William indignantly. "I've had enough bother over this an' it's all your fault, anyway. What did you go and *tell* him for? I was only makin' it up. I didn't do it. The other boy did it."

"You did it. You said so."

"Well, I was pretendin'. I was only jus' sayin' what the other boy had said."

"What other boy?"

"The boy what did it."

"Well, that's you. You *said* it was you."

"Oh, shut up," said William irritably. "I'm sick of arguing with you. You've got no sense. Girls never have. And let me tell you—"

He stopped abruptly. Rounding the bend in the road they had almost run into the Vicar's wife and a friend.

"Oh, here *is* Mrs. Hobbin," said the Vicar's wife, "so you can have a talk with her yourself." She gazed down the road after the figure of the little girl who had passed quickly on. "That was William Brown with you, wasn't it, Mrs Hobbin? I hope he wasn't teasing you in any way." She turned to her friend. "The little boy who's gone on down the road is a great trial to us all. My husband always calls him our village pest. Very rude and badly behaved, and a *great* nuisance in every way."

William, who had jerked his bonnet well over his eyes and drawn up his shawl well over his nose, glared ferociously at her through the narrow aperture. So the Vicar called him "our village pest", did he? He wouldn't forget that.

The Vicar's wife was looking at him with a perplexed frown. She'd broken her glasses that morning and had sent them off at once to be mended, but had not got them back yet. She hadn't realised before what a difference they made to people's sizes. Both William Brown and Mrs. Hobbin looked much smaller than when she wore her glasses. She couldn't see their features at all distinctly, of course, but that she was prepared for. What she wasn't prepared for was their looking so much smaller than they really were. Odd. Very odd. Perhaps she'd better visit her oculist again and consult him about it. It couldn't, of course, be anyone *but* Mrs. Hobbin. That violet-trimmed bonnet and all-enveloping shawl were famous in the neighbourhood. The old lady seemed to be trying to edge away, so the Vicar's wife laid a detaining hand on her arm.

"This friend of mine, dear Mrs. Hobbin," she said, "is writing a description of village characters, to be called 'Nature's Ladies and Gentlemen', and she has come over here for the day to interview some of you good old people. We were on our way to find you, as a matter of fact. . . ." She turned to her friend. "This dear old lady, Laetitia," she said, "is one of my greatest friends. She's seventy-eight, and she's never had a day's

illness in her life, have you, dear Mrs. Hobbin?"
William grimaced at her through the aperture. "She
comes regularly to our mothers' meetings and pleasant
Sunday afternoons, and takes part in all our little
outings. Now I'll leave you to have your little chat, and
I'll just go over there and rest my eyes. They seem to be
playing queer tricks with me just now."

She went over to the low wall just out of earshot and
sat on it, her eyes closed, smiling vaguely.

The visitor took out her note-book, gazing at William
in bewilderment. What a very strange old woman. One
couldn't see anything of her face at all. And how small.
Almost a dwarf. Curious that dear Elfrida hadn't mentioned that. Really not at all the sort of type she wanted
for "Nature's Ladies and Gentlemen". But still . . .

"Er—would you mind lowering your shawl a little?"
she said.

William made a hoarse noise, unmistakably indicative
of refusal. The perplexity of his interlocutor deepened.

"You—er—got a bad cold perhaps?" she suggested.

William made another hoarse noise, accepting the
suggestion.

"I expect that that's why you're so hoarse."

He croaked that it was. The authoress took her pencil.

"Now, dear Mrs. Hobbin," she said persuasively, "I
want you to tell me something about yourself. You're
seventy-eight years old, aren't you?"

William glanced up and down the road. His first
instinct had been flight from this hideous predicament,
but second thoughts counselled him to remain where he
was. Should Farmer Brewster, the policeman, or the
foreman come down the road seeking their prey they
would surely pass by this innocent little group—the
Vicar's wife seated on the wall, and, a short distance
away, her friend talking to dear old Mrs. Hobbin—

without suspicion. He decided to submit to the interview.

"How many children have you had?" said the authoress.

William tried to remember exactly how many children Mrs. Hobbin had. Certainly so many that she seemed to have peopled all the surrounding villages as well as her own.

"I've forgotten jus' how many," he croaked; "a good many."

"B-but," protested her surprised interviewer, "surely, dear Mrs. Hobbin, you remember how many children you have."

"I'm always meanin' to count 'em," croaked William, "but I keep on forgettin'."

The interviewer gaped at him helplessly. An explanation of the old lady's strange conduct suddenly occurred to her.

"Er—pardon me—Mrs. Hobbin," she said, "but—er—are you a teetotaller?"

"A what?" croaked William.

"I mean—do you *drink*—I mean, of course—er—moderately."

"Oh, yes, I drink all right," croaked William. "I drink a lot."

The interviewer laughed constrainedly.

"Fond of your glass?" she suggested faintly, with an unsuccessful attempt at a man-to-man air.

William, realising that he had no knowledge at all of Mrs. Hobbin's tastes and characteristics, decided to describe his own, considering that his own were as sensible and universal as any.

"No, not a glass," he croaked; "I like drinkin' out of a bottle best. I take a bottle in my pocket wherever I go."

The interviewer glanced beseechingly at the Vicar's wife, but the Vicar's wife was still sitting on the wall out of earshot, her eyes closed, smiling vaguely. The interviewer decided to change the subject.

"To what," she said, "do you attribute your longevity?"

"Uh?" said William.

"I mean how do you think it is that you've lived so much longer than—er—than some other people?"

"Jus' 'cause I've not died, I suppose," croaked William after deep thought.

The interviewer made a last and desperate effort.

"Now, Mrs. Hobbin," she said, "I want you to tell me something about yourself . . . your tastes and hobbies. What is your favourite food?"

"Ice-cream," croaked William promptly. "I c'n eat twenty ice-cream horns one after the other straight off."

The authoress shuddered.

"Your favourite occupation?"

"Goin' to fairs an' goin' on switchbacks an' havin' shots at Aunt Sally."

The authoress's cheeks blanched.

"Can you read?"

"Uh-huh."

"What sort of books do you like reading?"

"Plenty of fightin' an' people killin' people."

"You've had a hard life, Mrs. Hobbin?"

"Yes, I jolly well have," croaked William, thinking of his day's adventures.

"But you're at peace with the world now?"

"No, I've gotter lot of enemies."

"I'm sorry to hear that."

"I like havin' enemies," croaked William. "I like a jolly good fight. I gotter black eye only last week. But I jolly well made the other person's nose bleed all right."

The little girl had lingered for some time down the road waiting for him, but, suddenly tiring of waiting, had now set off briskly and was vanishing out of sight. William, seeing his suit disappearing, and realising that with it went his only chance of returning to ordinary life, mumbled a "'Scuse me", and set off in pursuit, repeating his attempt to combine a gait suitable to old age with as much speed as possible—an attempt that resulted in an odd, hopping step reminiscent of a kangaroo. The authoress watched him with an expression of helpless bewilderment till he was out of sight. Then she turned to her notes and read them through with shuddering horror. "Bottle in pocket." "People killin' people." "Gotter black eye last week."

What a *horrible* old woman! She considered for a moment whether to write up the notes and make from it the picture of a repulsive old battle-axe in the modern manner. But, no, that wasn't what her own particular public wanted of her, and one must give one's own particular public what one's own particular public wanted of one. She crossed out her notes and began to write again on a fresh page. "Mrs. Hobbin. This dear old lady spoke with touching affection of her many children and grandchildren, in all of whom she still takes a passionate interest. She is very abstemious in every way and is an ardent upholder of temperance, attributing her wonderful health chiefly to that. She can still do an active day's work but her chief pleasure is to sit in the porch of her little cottage, listening to the birds and watching her simple flowers. . . ."

Yes, thought the authoress with rising satisfaction, that's the sort of thing they want. Truth is, after all, the greater part of art; one must be true to what one's public wants.

The Vicar's wife rose and blinked and looked around her.

"Yes, they seem better now," she said. "They went so funny a minute ago. They made people look quite tiny. Extraordinary. I must consult my oculist about it. Mrs. Hobbin has gone, has she, dear?"

"Yes," said the friend, closing her note-book.

"A sweet old lady, isn't she?"

The friend hesitated for a moment. But already the memory of the actual interview was fading, and she saw quite vividly a dear old lady sitting in a cottage porch listening to the birds and watching her simple flowers.

"Sweet," she agreed with enthusiasm.

* * *

William had caught up with the little girl at the end of the lane leading to his home.

"Come along quickly into our summer-house an' give me my suit back," he said breathlessly. "I'm sick of goin' about in these things."

"But I *like* being a boy," she protested. "I want to go on being a boy. I don't want to give you back your suit. I want you to go to a foreign country like the man did in the book and let me go on wearing your suit and pretending I'm a boy."

"I've told you I'm *not* going to a foreign country," said William testily. "An' I'm sick of wearing these ole things an' ole women askin' me silly questions about liq'rice water an' ice-cream an' suchlike. Give me back my suit."

"But it's a *disguise*," persisted the little girl. "If I give you your suit back you won't be disguised any longer an' they'll take you to prison."

"Well, I don't care if they do. I'd rather go to prison than go on wearin' these ole things. Here's my house.

"COME ALONG QUICKLY INTO OUR SUMMER-HOUSE AND GIVE ME
MY SUIT BACK," SAID WILLIAM BREATHLESSLY.

Come into the summer-house an' give me my suit."

The little girl darted in at the gate and ran round the
side of the house shouting: "All right. . . . Catch me
first."

* * *

Mrs. Brown was entertaining a business friend of Mr. Brown's in the drawing-room. It was a business friend with whom Mr. Brown was hoping to make an advantageous business transaction, and, therefore, Mrs. Brown was doing her very best to put her visitor and his wife into a good humour. So far everything had gone well. William had not put in an appearance, for which William's mother was sincerely grateful.

"So delightful here in the country," said the visitor.

"Yes, isn't it," said Mrs. Brown. "We're all very fond of the country."

"You have a little boy, I believe?" went on the visitor.

"Yes," said Mrs. Brown.

"I love little boys. I'd love to meet him."

"I'm afraid he's out," said Mrs. Brown, aware that William was not the sort of little boy that people are thinking of when they say that they love little boys.

"Perhaps he'll come home before we go."

"I h— I mean I think not," said Mrs. Brown.

But the smile had died from her face, and a look of frozen horror had taken its place.

Out of the corner of her eye she had seen William return to the garden. She did not look at him directly because she did not wish to draw her visitor's attention to him, but the corner of her eye could not mistake that familiar grey tweed suit—originally advertised by its makers as "hard wearing", and already hard worn.

But it was not this that brought the frozen look of horror to Mrs. Brown's face. It was another familiar figure closely following the familiar figure of William. Again Mrs Brown dared not look directly at the figure for fear of drawing her visitors' attention to it, but even the corner of her eye recognised the violet-trimmed bonnet and voluminous shawl that belonged to Mrs.

Hobbin. What was Mrs. Hobbin doing here? She came
as a matter of course to help with the washing on
Monday morning—but this was not Monday morning.
And even on Monday morning Mrs. Hobbin did not
flaunt herself in the garden in this manner. What was
Mrs. Hobbin doing in the garden on a Thursday afternoon? The corner of Mrs. Brown's eye answered her.
She was chasing William—chasing William round and
round the lawn, in and out of the flower-beds. What on
earth had William been doing now? At all costs the
visitors' eyes must be kept from the horrible spectacle.
She rose abruptly and went to the opposite window that
looked out upon the front garden.

"D-d-do look at the view from here," she said, "we—
we think it so pretty."

The visitors rose and joined her at the window—
gazing in a bewildered fashion at the front garden and
the path by which they had come in. There was nothing
in the front garden except a lawn encircled by laurel
bushes. Beyond the hedge was an extremely dull stretch
of country road.

"Yes, isn't it?" said the visitors dutifully but without
enthusiasm, preparing to return to their seats.

"Such pretty er—bushes," went on Mrs. Brown
frantically, gazing at her laurel bushes, "and the road's
so pretty just here."

"Er—yes," said the visitors, glancing at her
curiously.

But the corner of Mrs. Brown's eye had told her that
those two strange figures had stopped chasing each other
round the back garden, and she was just about to resume
her seat with a sigh of relief, when she saw an equally
strange company coming down the road. First came
Farmer Brewster, then a policeman, then Mr. Greg, and
then—Mrs. Brown put her hand to her head—yes, it *was*

Mrs. Hobbin, Mrs. Hobbin bare-headed, wearing an apron, her sleeves rolled above her elbows, Mrs. Hobbin her face set in grim, angry lines, marching to battle, arms akimbo. Two Mrs. Hobbins—one in the front garden, one in the back; one with a shawl and bonnet, one without. . . . But Mrs. Brown had no time to puzzle over the strange problem.

Farmer Brewster was opening the gate of the Brown garden. The procession entered.

"HERE'S THE BOY, CONSTABLE," SAID FARMER BREWSTER. THE POLICEMAN TOOK OUT HIS NOTE-BOOK.

"Excuse me," said Mrs. Brown faintly, "I think these people want to speak to me. . . ."

Suddenly, from nowhere as it seemed, William and a little girl appeared. He had offered her his catapult as well as the cigarette cards and whistle, and she had at last consented to return his suit. The exchange had been effected quickly in the summer-house and now William strutted about, exulting in his newly regained manhood, and the little girl drooped disconsolately in the pink cotton frock. The shawl and violet-trimmed bonnet lay discarded on the floor of the summer-house. Mrs Hobbin

"AND WHO," DEMANDED MRS. HOBBIN STRIDENTLY OF MRS. BROWN, "SENDS THEIR BOYS OUT STEALING RESPECTABLE WOMEN'S CLOTHES?"

at the front door, gazing grimly through the open garden door beyond, espied them suddenly and flung herself through the house and into the summer-house. From there she emerged wearing not only her familiar shawl and bonnet but the look of one who thirsts for vengeance. The procession had followed her into the back garden. Mrs. Brown, in helpless bewilderment, accompanied them. The visitors followed still more helplessly bewildered, thinking that somehow they must have got mixed up with a cinema show.

"Here's the boy, constable," said Farmer Brewster, once more applying the grip of iron to William's neck.

The policeman took out his note-book.

"And who," demanded Mrs. Hobbin stridently of Mrs. Brown, "sends their boys out stealing respectable women's clothes?"

"That's not the boy," said the foreman, looking at William. "That's not the boy that played those pranks on our farm. The boy that did that looked quite different. He'd got red hair for one thing."

Farmer Brewster pulled William's hair experimentally. It remained its own nondescript colour. Disappointed of his prey, he began to argue furiously with his foreman. Everyone in fact was arguing furiously with someone. The policeman was arguing with Farmer Brewster and Farmer Brewster was arguing with his foreman and his foreman was arguing with Mrs. Brown and Mrs. Brown was arguing with Mrs. Hobbin and Mrs. Hobbin was arguing with everyone else.

Under cover of this general argument, William crept quietly away.

Chapter 12

It All Began with the Typewriter

William trudged thoughtfully down the road, his hands in his pockets, a bar of liquorice stuck pipewise in his mouth, his cap, as usual, over one eye, his tie, as if trying to preserve a certain symmetry, under the other ear.

William was thinking deeply. This day next week would be the 14th February—Saint Valentine's Day. The occasion would have meant nothing to William if his mother had not the night before shown him a collection of valentines that had been sent to his grandmother in her youth—elaborate affairs of red velvet hearts on white lace background, of pressed and gilded ferns, of love scenes hand-painted upon lustrous satin, of discreetly amorous ditties surrounded by corpulent cupids or pierced hearts.

William, deeply impressed by these masterpieces and fired by a longing to emulate the makers of them, had "borrowed" the red ink from Robert's bureau. He found that he could make excellent pierced hearts with it. Moreover, the process was a distinctly pleasant one. William had always enjoyed having dealings of any kind with red ink. He outlined the hearts first, then filled them in by splashes of red ink. When the splashes went over the outline he enlarged the outline till in the end the hearts assumed odd, sausage-like contours that would have much puzzled any student of anatomy. William, however, was completely satisfied with them. He decided to decorate a page of his mother's best notepaper with them and to write his love motto in the middle. The love motto he had decided upon was:

"So fair you are, so fair and sweet,
I lay my heart down at your feet."

He practised writing this upon a piece of rough paper, but even William, optimist as he was, realised that his writing fell far below the high standard of calligraphy set by his grandmother's admirers. He wrote it several times, but each time the resultant blots seemed to become more numerous. William had long ago resigned himself to the fact that any pen wielded by him shed blots on all sides as freely as a thunder cloud sheds rain. Generally he had no great objection to this, as he prided himself upon the skill with which by the addition of a few legs he could turn his blots into spiders or beetles, according to their shape. But there was enough of the artist in him to appreciate the fact that beetles and spiders were incompatible with pierced hearts. No, this motto must not be adorned by beetles or spiders. It must be beautifully written and free of such extraneous ornaments. He tried it ten times, tore up each effort in disgust, and was just beginning to despair when suddenly, walking down the road, pondering over the problem and chewing his liquorice, he remembered Robert's typewriter.

Robert's typewriter was a new acquisition, and Robert guarded it zealously, especially from William. He kept it generally carefully locked in its case, but William, who took a deep and scientific interest in it, had on more than one occasion managed to obtain access to it, and had carried out several interesting experiments upon it. After the last experiment Robert had had to return the machine to the makers to be put into working order again. William, therefore, had been strictly forbidden even to look at the typewriter after that. But William argued with himself that it could not possibly do it any harm just to type one sentence with it. After all, that was what it was for. He would only just keep it in practice when Robert wasn't using it. It would be a kindness to Robert just to do that. And he felt that a typewritten motto would once and for all settle the question of the superiority of his valentine over his grandmother's, which were all either printed or written. He had not yet decided to whom he would send it. That, he considered, was a mere detail compared with the making of it.

He hurried home and crept slowly and cautiously up to Robert's bedroom. The door was open, and the room was empty. Empty of Robert, that is, but not of the typewriter. The typewriter stood on the table by the window. There were no sounds anywhere in the house. He tiptoed into the bedroom and to the table. There was a piece of paper already inserted, with some typing on it. William could not resist the temptation to try his motto at once. When he had tried it, he would take out the paper. If Robert questioned him as to its disappearance he would try to persuade him that it must have blown out of the window. Robert could easily do his bit of typing again. His fingers hovered over the keys, then crashed down. It took him some time, but the result was, on the whole, fairly satisfactory:

> Sofair you? are%. SO fairand sweet.
> ilay my heart down¾ at youR feet.

He gazed at it in pride for a few moments and was just putting out his hand to roll the paper off when he heard a

footstep on the stairs. It was Robert's footstep; there
was no mistaking it. He had not heard the front door
open or any sound in the hall, but it was certainly
Robert's footstep on the stairs. Without stopping to
remove the sheet of paper, he slipped out of Robert's
bedroom into his own.

Robert entered his bedroom and closed the door.
William waited anxiously for the outburst of fury that
should mark Robert's discovery of his unauthorised use
of the typewriter. But no outburst came. . . . The
luncheon bell rang and Robert emerged from his room,
looking thoughtful, but, on the whole, quite amicable.
Obviously he had not yet discovered the valentine.
William followed him down the stairs, wearing an
expression of mingled caution and virtue.

"I've been out playin' till jus' this minute," he
announced loudly to no one in particular, with the vague
hope of establishing an alibi should it prove necessary.

But Robert was too deeply taken up by his own affairs
to have any thought for William's. He was a youth of
great susceptibility and was just now in the ticklish
process of being off with the old love and on with the
new. He was, as a matter of fact, so completely off with
the old love that the old love was now engaged to
someone else, but he was not yet completely on with the
new. The root of Robert's trouble, of course, was that he
frequented the "pictures" and fell in love regularly with
the star who took the principal part in every film he saw.
He had fallen in love with Cornelia Gerrard because she
reminded him of Greta Garbo, but a few weeks later he
went to see a film featuring Marlene Dietrich, with the
result that he had decided that Cornelia was not his type,
after all, but that Lorna Barton, whose profile really had
a distinct look of Marlene Dietrich, was his true soul's
mate. As far as Cornelia Gerrard was concerned, the

affair was simple enough, for Cornelia had tired of
Robert long before Robert had tired of her and was now
actually engaged to a young man called Peter Greenham, who reminded her of Maurice Chevalier, and
simply couldn't imagine why on earth she'd ever thought
that Robert was like Ronald Colman. But with regard to
Lorna Barton the affair was more complicated. For
Lorna, fully aware of her charms, was as capricious and
exacting as the heroine of a Victorian novel. A large
company of admirers bore witness to her attractions.
Robert found himself in the unenviable position of an
"also ran".

The situation put him on his mettle, and he lost no
time in finding out the beloved's weak spots. The chief
among them, he discovered, was a regard for
appearances. . . . She attended chiefly films in which
well-dressed heroines move perpetually in luxurious
interiors, among crowds of well-dressed admirers. She
longed to be surrounded continually by elegant, tall,
slender males, clad in immaculate morning suits and top
hats. She cherished a secret passion for top hats, and not
one of her actual admirers possessed one. The ward-
robes, in fact, of the youths of the neighbourhood
seemed to consist solely of shapeless grey flannel
trousers and equally shapeless pull-overs. They
generally went about without hats, but when they wore
these appendages they were, if possible, even more
shapeless than the rest of their outfits. Robert first rose
from the ruck of the main body of her admirers by
appearing at a local wedding in a top hat.

The top hat belonged to his father, who had originally
bought it for his own wedding. It was midway between a
family pet and a family heirloom, and was always
referred to by the Browns as Ermyntrude. Mr. Brown
guarded her zealously and, until the occasion of the local

wedding, had always firmly refused to lend her to Robert. And the occasion had not been an unqualified success, for Robert had put her upon a chair at the wedding reception, and Mr. Bott, who was both stout and short-sighted, had inadvertently sat down upon her. Robert had done his best to repair the damage, but Mr. Brown had seen at once that she had lost an undue amount of what gloss and shape the passing years had left her. He had stroked her with tender solicitude and had said firmly: "Never again, my boy. You can ask till you're black in the face; I'll never lend her to you again."

But Robert realised that he made great strides in the estimation of his beloved, and he was well aware that it was all owing to Ermyntrude.

He was not, therefore, surprised the next week when she said to him: "Robert, I've been asked to a musical At Home at Marleigh Grange, and I've got them to ask you, too, so that you can take me there." Then she looked him up and down in a speculative manner and added: "You'll wear your top hat for it, won't you, Robert?"

And Robert, in whose eyes her likeness to Marlene Dietrich seemed to grow more striking every time he saw her, smiled and said: "Of course", as if the idea of not going to a musical At Home in a top hat had never even occurred to him.

He threw out a tentative hint to his father that evening, but his father was adamant.

"No, my boy," he said; "you put ten years on to Ermyntrude's life the last time you had her, and you're not having her again till my funeral, so you can take that as final." A lifetime's experience had taught Robert that it was a waste of time to argue with his father. The only solution of the problem, therefore, was to obtain

possession of Ermyntrude without his father's knowledge. This, of course, would not be easy. Her size and
shape made it difficult to secrete her about one's person,
and his mother would be sure to want to inspect his final
appearance with maternal pride on the day he set off to
the musical At Home.

He was deeply absorbed in the problem as he walked
downstairs to lunch in front of William. He had not even
looked at the paper on which William had typed his
valentine motto. As a matter of fact, the paper was a
letter to the old love, Cornelia Gerrard. Robert, of
course, did not want to write to her. The Greta Garbo
type now inspired in him only an amused contempt.
Moreover, he realised that the less one has to do with an
ex-beloved who is engaged to someone else the better
for all concerned. But as secretary of the local Badminton club he had been deputed to write and ask Miss
Gerrard if she would take charge, as usual, of the
refreshments at the annual dance that was the chief
reason for the Badminton club's existence.

Robert's letter was coldly formal and correct. His
somewhat erratic typing detracted a little from its
dignity, perhaps, but in spite of that it was obviously not
meant to be a friendly letter.

Dear½ Miss Gerrarxd" . . .
        I am% requestedby the commitTee of the Bad-
minton Club to ask youif—you will beso! good as to"
supervise the refreshments at our annual & dance as y-
ou so kindlydid last 9 year½."

He had been called away at that point before he had
had time to close the letter. William's added line was, of
course, in keeping with the typography, if not the
sentiment, of the letter as a whole.

Both Robert and William were silent during lunch. Robert was still absorbed in the problem of Ermyntrude. It seemed equally impossible to obtain possession of her and to go to the musical At Home without her. An early death, Robert decided, was really the only solution. His father would wear Ermyntrude at his funeral and wish that he hadn't been so mean about her. Lorna, looking more like Marlene Dietrich than ever, would weep into his grave.

William was feeling slightly nervous about the valentine with which he had inadvertently presented Robert. He decided to lie in wait in his own bedroom and, as soon as the coast was clear, to slip in and take out the paper before Robert found it. To his dismay Robert went straight up to his bedroom after lunch. William hung about the side door, ready to take to his heels should Robert discover the valentine, or to slip up to Robert's room to retrieve the paper should Robert leave it, still in ignorance of the outrage.

Robert, in his bedroom, looked with distaste at the paper in the typewriter. It was that wretched letter to that wretched girl. He couldn't think what he'd ever seen in Greta Garbo anyway. He hoped that she'd realise from the extreme coldness of the letter that he'd finished with her for ever, and that he was jolly glad she'd got engaged to Peter Greenham and jolly sorry for *him*. He had finished it all but just the ending. Without reading it through again he typed; "Yours truly" (Yes, truly. That ought to make her feel jolly small), "R? Brown," took it off the roller, folded it up, fastened it into an envelope, addressed it, and went downstairs. William was hanging about at the side door. He'd send the kid with it and save a halfpenny.

"I'll give you a penny if you'll take this letter," he said loftily.

"Right," said William, who never despised a penny and knew that it was economically impossible to obtain more than a penny for delivering a letter by hand.

He ran along the road quickly, pretending that he was a spy carrying despatches through an enemy's country and that the hedge was alive with hostile spies, trying to shoot him. Occasionally he flung himself full length upon the ground in order to avoid the imaginary bullets that whizzed around him. Sometimes he crawled along the ditch—much to the detriment of his personal appearance—in an attempt to mislead his imaginary pursuers. He did not, of course, hurry. At the back of his mind was a vague idea that by taking a good time over the errand he would ensure that on his return Robert would either have gone out for a walk, leaving the coast clear, or, if he had discovered William's use of his typewriter, would have had time to get over the first shock of his fury.

He reached the house at last and ran up the drive to the front door, half expecting—so real had the imaginary adventure become to him—to see a magnificently uniformed general issue from the front door to receive the despatches. Instead he saw Cornelia in the conservatory, and the sight brought him back to reality.

Becoming an ordinary boy again, he entered the conservatory and stood there for a moment in the doorway. Cornelia was not alone, and one glance told William (who himself possessed a temperamental sister) that a ffrst-class scene was in progress. The other—and passive—participant in it was Peter Greenham, her fiancé, who stood sulkily receiving the torrents of her wrath.

"Forgot!" she shrilled, obviously repeating an excuse he had just made. "Forgot! I like that. There I was waiting and *waiting*, and you never came."

Muttering, he repeated the excuse that was evidently so much worse than the fault it excused.

"Well, I forgot. I'd been playing Rugger all afternoon and I was dead tired and so I went to bed early and I forgot that I'd promised to take you to the pictures."

Speech failed her for a few moments, then she appealed wildly to a rather decrepit-looking palm that grew at a rakish angle from its plant pot.

"Did you hear that?" she said. "He forgot! *Forgot!*" Even the palm seemed to wilt slightly at the scorn in her voice. "He forgot, if you please. And that's the man I'm

ONE GLANCE TOLD WILLIAM THAT A FIRST-CLASS SCENE WAS IN PROGRESS.

going to marry. Look at him!" The palm looked at him and, assisted by a slight draught from the open door, waved a raggy tentacle at him derisively.

"Forgot!" repeated the girl who seemed to find the

CORNELIA DREW OFF HER RING. "TAKE THAT," SHE SAID DRAMATICALLY. "I DON'T WANT TO RISK BEING *FORGOTTEN* BY YOU ANY MORE."

repetition effective. "*Forgot!* I suppose he'd *forget* to turn up for the wedding. He'd *forget* to find a house for me or give me any money to keep it on. He'd—" Once more rage choked her. She drew off her ring with a convulsive gesture and handed it to him. "Take that," she said dramatically. "I don't want to risk being *forgotten* by you any more."

"Look here," said the youth. "Don't be such a darned little fool—"

"That's right," screamed the girl. "Swear at me—"

She turned suddenly and saw William, who was still standing, an interested spectator, in the doorway. "Well," she said sharply, "what do *you* want?"

"I've brought a note from Robert," said William, flinching from the fury of her gaze. "I think it wants an answer."

She snatched it from him and tore it open as viciously as if it, too, had forgotten to take her to the pictures. Then she read it. . . .

William, who was by now deeply interested in the situation, shifted his position and craned his neck so as to see as much as possible of Robert's letter. As soon as his eyes fell on it they bulged with sudden dismay. There was his valentine. . . .

He realised the awful truth. He had typed it in the middle of a letter of Robert's, and Robert had finished the letter without seeing what he had done. . . .

He opened his mouth to explain, but already Cornelia was flourishing the letter triumphantly in Peter's face.

"And do you know what this is?" she demanded.

"No," said Peter, backing away from her, "and I don't want to eat the thing, anyway."

"Well, it's a proposal of marriage from someone else," went on the outraged damsel, "and I'm going to accept it. You think you can treat me like *dirt*, leaving

me standing hours and *hours* outside picture houses—
well, you're not the only man in the world though you
seem to think you are, and I'm going to accept this other
man and jolly well never going to *speak* to you again.
I've *finished* with you."

She snatched up the microscopic circle of crochet
work that did service as her hat, and rammed it viciously
upon her head.

"Here, where are you going?" said the youth.

"I'm going to tell this other man I'll marry him," said
Cornelia, still white with fury, "and you can find
someone else to keep waiting for you hours and *hours*
outside picture houses, and I hope I never see you again.
So there!"

With that she flounced away, almost running down the
drive to the gate. The young man hurried after her, but
the more he hurried the faster she went, till a passer-by
would have thought that he was actually chasing the girl
down the road. Realising this, he shrugged his shoulders
and turned off in the opposite direction. William,
however, continued the pursuit. He felt that at all costs
he must explain the situation to her before she found
Robert. . . . He caught her up and said breathlessly:

"Please jus' listen to me a minute—"

She waved him from her.

"I can't listen to you now," she said. "I have other
things to think of. You're a very tiresome little boy to
come bothering me like this. . . . Go *away!*"

She stamped her foot at him.

"But, listen," said William desperately. "It's about
that letter—"

But at that moment there appeared round the bend in
the road the figure of Robert, carrying a large bandbox.

Robert looked pale and anxious. He was making a
bold effort to secure Ermyntrude for the musical At

Home. Ermyntrude, in fact, reposed in the bandbox. Robert had abstracted her from his father's wardrobe and put her in the bandbox. He had then told his mother that he was going to offer to lend his fancy dress costume (a slightly anachronistic representation of Charles I) to Jameson Jameson, and had boldly walked out of the house carrying the bandbox, under the fond maternal eye.

"So kind of you, dear," she had murmured, "so few boys would have thought of it. . . ." So far, so good, of course; but the path was still beset with dangers. He intended to leave the hat in Jameson Jameson's keeping till the day of the At Home, letting him fully into the plot. At present, fortunately, Jameson Jameson was passing through a woman-hater phase and was refusing all invitations to functions at which women were to be present. He would regard the whole affair with superior and tolerant amusement. But his woman-hating phases generally ended very abruptly in complete enslavement to some local beauty, and there was always the possibility that this one would end before the musical At Home, and that he would not be able to resist the temptation of purloining Ermyntrude for his own embellishment. Still—the plan was the best that Robert could devise on the spur of the moment. His mind was fully occupied with the problem as he came down the road, and he was just going to pass Cornelia with an absent nod when she stopped in front of him.

"Robert," she said dramatically, "I've come to say 'Yes'."

Robert stared at her in astonishment, then suddenly remembered the letter he had just despatched to her asking her to supervise the refreshments for the Badminton club dance.

"Oh, good," he said absently, and was preparing to

walk on again when she put out her hand as if to hold him off.

"Don't kiss me, Robert," she said.

"No," he said feebly. "No, I wasn't going to."

She continued, the tragedy of her manner gaining in

SHE PUT UP HER HAND AS IF TO HOLD HIM OFF. "DON'T KISS ME, ROBERT," SHE SAID.

dramatic value every moment, till it would have done credit to Lady Macbeth herself.

"I say 'yes', Robert, but my heart is not in this. I want you to know that my heart is not in it. My heart is cold and dead. I've been so terribly, terribly hurt that I shall never feel anything, *anything*, all the rest of my life. . . . I want it to be kept a secret for the present. Will you agree to that?"

"Oh, yes," said Robert, still deeply bewildered. "Oh yes, it can be kept a secret if you like. . . ."

After all, there wasn't any need for anyone to know that she was in charge of the refreshments if she didn't want them to. No, she certainly wasn't a bit like Greta Garbo. He didn't know why he'd ever thought she was.

"And—as it's being kept a secret, there's no need of a ring just for the present, of course."

"A what?" said Robert.

"A ring. I needn't wear a ring."

Robert gaped at her in helpless amazement.

"Oh, no," he said, "of course you needn't. Just wear what you like."

He had a vague idea the ladies presiding over the refreshments wore a sort of badge on their dress, but he'd never heard of them wearing any special sort of ring. Perhaps it was some modern idea. She'd always been like that—up to date and superior and trying to make everyone else feel as if they'd come out of the ark. No, he certainly couldn't think what he'd ever seen in her.

"Oh, no," he said loftily, "there's no need at all of a ring in the circumstances."

"And I want you to understand fully that my *heart* isn't in it."

"Oh, yes, that's quite all right," said Robert, "as long as you'll do it."

He was feeling nervous lest she should begin to question him about this bandbox. She'd always been able to worm things out of him. . . .

He held the bandbox firmly behind his back and smiled foolishly. She uttered a hollow laugh.

"Oh, yes," she said, "I'll go through with it. Though my heart's like a *stone*, I'll go through with it."

"That's quite all right," said Robert vaguely.

"And now please leave me," she said with an imperious wave of her hand.

Much relieved, Robert trotted on down the road with his bandbox, and Cornelia went on her way, her brow drawn into a frown of tragic intensity as she composed the letter in which she should inform Peter Greenham that she was now engaged to someone else. She would not tell him the name, of course. She would merely say that it was someone who would *not* keep her waiting hours and *hours* outside picture houses. . . . Her spirits rose slightly as she composed the letter. That would *show* him. . . . And if she met him she'd simply stare at him as if she'd never seen him before. That would show him, too.

In preparation for the contingency she took out her vanity case and carefully powdered her nose, assuming her most Greta Garboish expression as she did so. . . .

After a discreet interval William climbed out of the ditch from which he had been listening to the conversation. He fully realised the situation and was uneasily aware that his misguided attempt at typing his "motto" was responsible for it. He realised, moreover, that the situation had gone beyond the point at which it could be set right by a confession of his unauthorised use of Robert's typewriter.

He had for his age a fairly good knowledge of human nature. If he confessed to Cornelia she would refuse to

believe the story and would make one of her famous
"scenes" with Robert over it. If he confessed to Robert,
Robert would not only exact vengeance from him, but
would still regard himself as bound by honour to the
jilted damsel to whom he had so inadvertently proposed.
For Robert had been brought up on the best romantic
fiction, and knew that a real gentleman never breaks off
his engagement to a lady even though he only got
engaged to her by accident.

For the rest of the morning William grappled with the
problem, and it was not till the middle of lunch that a
solution presented itself.

So simple and perfect a solution did it seem that he
wondered it had not occurred to him before. It was
nothing more or less than to make Cornelia believe that
Robert was already married. That, of course, would
automatically cancel the engagement. She would have
nothing more to do with Robert once she heard that he
was already married, and everything would be just as it
had been before his fatal tampering with the typewriter.

The only question was how to make her believe that
Robert was already married. William had a wholesome
awe of the lady herself. Then he remembered her
sister—Angela—a schoolgirl of about thirteen. One
could tell Angela anything without any danger of her
rage, for Angela was afraid of mice and fled shrieking
with terror from spiders. And Angela would be sure to
tell Cornelia, for it was notorious that Angela could
keep nothing to herself. Though of such tender years she
had in her all the makings of one of the world's finest
gossips.

William sauntered casually down the lane where the
Gerrards lived and there, by an unexpected stroke of
luck, met Angela strolling aimlessly along, sucking a
large bull's-eye, her pale eyes fixed on the horizon.

"Hello," said William.

Angela's pale eyes dropped from the horizon to William. She shifted her bull's-eye from one cheek to the other.

"Hello!" she replied vaguely.

"I've got a secret," said William.

Angela's pale eyes gleamed.

"Tell it me," she pleaded.

"No, I can't," said William, playing his fish with care. "I tell you it's a secret."

Angela drew a packet of bull's-eyes from her pocket and handed it to William.

"Take two," she said.

William selected the three largest and put them in his mouth.

"Go on," pleaded Angela, "tell me."

William made an unintelligible sound and pointed to his mouth. The bull's-eyes were unusually large ones and for the time being deprived him of speech, even, almost, of breath.

"I said *two*," murmured Angela reproachfully.

William made a spirited sound that was evidently meant to justify his action and at the same time accuse her of meanness. They walked down the lane in silence till William by skilful manipulation had reduced the unruly mouthful to subjection.

"Gotter secret," he said again indistinctly.

"Go on. Tell me," pleaded Angela again. "I gave you three bull's-eyes. You *might* tell me."

"You only gave me two," William reminded her. "I took the other."

"Well, I *let* you take it. Go on. Tell me, William."

"I can't tell you," said William, "it's a secret. But you'd be *jolly* surprised if you knew." This goaded Angela's curiosity to fever pitch. She began her famous process of worming out the secret.

"Is it about a person?" she said.

"Y-yes," said William, as if reluctantly. "Y-yes, it's about a person all right."

"Is it a him or a her?"

"It's a him," said William.

"What letter does his name begin with?" demanded Angela breathlessly.

"R," said William, "and he's in my family."

"*Robert!*" screamed Angela, swallowing a half-sucked bull's-eye in her excitement.

"Yes," said William simply, "it was jolly clever of you to guess it."

Angela struggled nobly with her choking fit. Though on the point of asphyxia, she fixed her streaming eyes on William with gimlet-like eagerness.

"What s-s-sort of a s-s-secret is it?" she gasped as soon as she could speak.

"I'll tell you if you'll promise not to tell anyone," said William.

"I promise, William. Go on, *do* tell me."

"Well, he's married."

She stared at him, bewildered and disappointed.

"But he *isn't* married," she objected. "I *know* he isn't married. There'd have been a wedding if he'd been married, and he'd have gone to live in a house of his own."

"Yes, but he's secretly married," explained William, sinking his voice to a confidential whisper. "No one but me knows about it. He got married in London, and his wife lives there an' he jus' goes up to see her sometimes. He pretends not to be married and goes on livin' at home, but I found out, so he told me all about it an' made me promise not to tell anyone, so you won't tell anyone, will you?"

"Oo, no," promised Angela glibly, her eyes agog.

"On your honour and cross your throat?" said William, aware that to Angela this formula would make the secret all the more important and the more worthy, therefore, of being divulged to suitable recipients.

"On my honour and cross my throat," gabbled Angela, and, her pale eyes protruding with eagerness, hurried off down the road to hand on the story as quickly as possible. . . .

* * *

The musical At Home was in full swing. Robert's manoeuvre had been entirely successful. He had gone to Jameson Jameson's and exchanged his trilby for Ermyntrude. Jameson Jameson's woman-hating phase still continued. It had reached, in fact, its acute stage, and he watched Robert's anxious preparation of his toilet with cynical amusement.

"Funny to think that I once cared for girls," he said with a superior smile, as he watched Robert carefully polishing Ermyntrude's somewhat lack-lustre nap.

"I used to feel like you when I was younger, of course," said Robert coldly, referring with deliberate malice to his month's seniority over Jameson. Jameson retorted by a sardonic laugh and they parted coldly—Jameson to continue a poem that he had begun that morning, called "The Curse of Woman", Robert to call for Lorna.

* * *

Lorna received him kindly and, walking with him along the road to Marleigh, made herself more pleasant than he had ever known her. She obviously approved of his appearance.

"I do think it makes such a difference, a top hat," she said.

"I do, too," agreed Robert complacently.

"I do so like a man to be well turned out," she went on.

"Yes, I do, too," agreed Robert.

"It makes such a difference, I think," she continued.

"So do I," said Robert.

"A top hat especially."

"Yes, I think so, too."

Even Robert, devoted, as he was, had to admit that her conversational powers were limited, but with a Marlene Dietrich profile conversational powers are, after all, superfluous.

"I think that *everyone* ought to be well turned out," she went on, with the air of one who propounds a startling and recondite truth.

"So do I," said Robert.

"I always take trouble to look well turned out. I'm not pretty, but—"

She paused for the expected outburst of contradiction. It did not fail her.

"Pretty!" echoed Robert so fervently that Ermyntrude—a poor fit at the best of times—almost engulfed him completely. "Pretty! Why, you're beautiful—*beautiful*. . . . You're the most beautiful girl I've ever seen in my life. Why—I've never seen anyone half as beautiful as you, ever. Ever in my whole life."

Lorna fluttered her Marlene Dietrich eyelashes at him and murmured:

"Oh, no—I'm *quite* plain really. *Quite*."

For the rest of her walk, Robert assured her with ever-increasing fervour that she was the most beautiful girl he had ever seen. Ever in his whole life.

In the hall of the Grange he handed Ermyntrude to

the maid-servant with a gesture worthy of a Hollywood duke, and followed Lorna into the concert room, feeling without Ermyntrude like a shorn Samson. But even though he now lacked the outward and visible sign of his superiority, still Lorna continued to be very nice to him, turning to him continually during the concert to ask him if he liked eye-veils, if he didn't think that earrings made Gloria Tompkins look frightfully common, and if he didn't think that Cornelia Gerrard was absolutely hideous. To the last Robert agreed fervently, and added that she was very strange. He said that he'd had to ask her to take charge of the refreshments at the Badminton club dance and she'd been very strange about it. Frightfully, in fact. At this point a music lover just in front of them turned round and glared so fiercely that Lorna did not speak again for nearly two minutes.

It was during the tea interval that Robert, left alone by Lorna who had joined a group of her friends, first began to notice something strange in the atmosphere.

People stood about in groups whispering together and watching him. One or two people whom he addressed seemed embarrassed and edged away from him. He could not know, of course, that the story of his secret marriage was gradually percolating through the company. Angela, on her way home to tell the story to Cornelia, had met Miss Amelia Blake and had not been able to resist imparting the news to her. Already the story had acquired various circumstantial details. The couple had been seen coming out of the registrar's office together. William had found the marriage certificate by accident in Robert's wallet. . . . Some said that his wife was an actress, others a housemaid.

Excitement increased as a further rumour reached them—a rumour brought by Emmeline Moston, who had had it from Cornelia herself—that Cornelia had that

morning broken off her engagement to Peter Greenham
and accepted Robert. The consternation and horror
with which they watched Robert increased. So might the
neighbours of Charles Peace have watched him had they
suddenly discovered his real character in the middle of a
musical At Home.

"And Heaven only knows," murmured Miss Gregoria Mutch faintly, "how many more of them he's
married and got engaged to. It's just like the Brides in
the Bath case. . . . Grown up among us and always
seemed so innocent, but, of course, that was his
cunning. . . ."

Robert's conscience stirred uneasily as he noticed the
looks that were being cast upon him. It would be just like
Jameson to have told people that Ermyntrude really
belonged to his father and that he'd not only taken her
without permission but after having been expressly
forbidden to take her. Mrs. Bruce-Monkton-Bruce
would never be looking at him in that grim, disapproving
way if she hadn't been told about Ermyntrude. . . . It
was a rotten trick of Jameson's and he'd jolly well get
even with him. . . . Yes, Mrs. Gerald Fitzgerald was
looking at him in just the same way. Jameson *must* have
told. . . .

He went back to the concert room. Lorna didn't
return to her seat and he found himself next to an elderly
woman with a very sharp elbow who nudged him and
said "Sh!" whenever he turned over his programme or
moved his feet. He was much relieved when the end of
the concert came.

He rescued Ermyntrude and went to wait for Lorna at
the bottom of the drive. He stood back from the gate
staring with set gaze above the heads of the people who
passed him, trying to avoid their gaze. Yes, they
certainly *were* looking at him in an odd way. He couldn't

help noticing it. He'd never speak to Jameson again. *Never*. His whole life would be ruined if the story got about. *Everyone* would be laughing at him. It wasn't even as if Ermyntrude were a really good fit. She came right down to his ears and once people got to know that she was his father's—well, he'd never live it down, and his whole life would be ruined. . . .

Everyone had come out now but Lorna, and he was left alone at the gate. Ah, here she was. . . . *She* was looking at him in an odd way, too. More than odd. In fact, he wilted visibly beneath the fury of her gaze.

"I've just heard something about you," she said icily. "I suppose you can guess what it is."

Robert hung his head guiltily.

"Yes," he admitted, "but just let me explain. It was—"

She cut him short with a sweeping wave of her arm.

"Don't dare to try to excuse yourself," she stormed. "Didn't you tell me that I was the most beautiful girl you'd ever met? Didn't you tell me you thought Cornelia Gerrard hideous?"

"Yes," stammered the bewildered Robert, 'but—"

"And then I hear *this*," she flamed, "and it wasn't as if it was only Cornelia. *Oh!*" She clenched her fists and gave a shudder of mingled horror and disgust. "You bigamist!" With that she swung on her heel and left him.

He gazed after her in helpless dismay, then slowly began to wend his way towards Jameson's house. After all, there surely wasn't anything to make such an awful scene about. But there was no doubt that girls made scenes over the merest trifles. . . . Look at the way Cornelia had gone on this morning simply because he'd asked her to take charge of the refreshments at the Badminton dance, and now here was Lorna going on even worse just because she'd found out that he'd borrowed his father's top hat. He really thought that it would be less trouble on the whole to be a woman-hater like Jameson. . . .

Meantime two conversations were taking place that concerned him nearby and that, had he heard them, would have increased his bewilderment.

Cornelia was sobbing in Peter Greenham's arms.

"Darling," she was saying, "I've had such a lesson. I'll never break off our engagement again. Yes, darling, I do quite forgive you for forgetting about the pictures, and I promise I'll never refer to it again—but all the same I simply can't *think* how you came to forget. We'd arranged it all most particularly, and it simply shows how little you cared about me to—"

"Yes, darling," said Peter soothingly. "Never mind that just now. You've got all the rest of our lives to talk about it. Tell me what happened. *Who's* insulted you?"

"I *told* you. That *awful* boy. He proposed to me this morning and I accepted him because—well, I naturally thought you didn't care for me. How can a man *possibly* care for a girl who he keeps waiting hours and hours and *hours* outside a picture house? I mean, it *shows* that you never loved me. If—"

"Yes, darling, but never mind that. How was it insulting you to propose to you?"

"I keep trying to *tell* you, but you keep interrupting every *second*. How can I tell you things when you're *perpetually* interrupting?"

"Sorry, darling."

"I've forgotten where I'd got to now with you interrupting so much."

"Someone proposed to you."

"Oh, yes, Robert Brown. Proposed to me and I accepted, not because I loved him but because I felt that my heart was *dead*. You'd hurt me so *dreadfully*. I mean

you do see how you hurt me, don't you? I'm not one to
keep harping on a thing, but you must see that to keep a
girl waiting hours and *hours* outside a—"

"Yes, darling—well, get on to where he insulted
you."

"I wish you wouldn't keep hurrying me so. I'm *trying*
to tell you. Well, I accepted him and then—oh, I can
hardly tell you—I find that the brute was secretly
married all the time."

Peter stared at her in amazement.

"*Married!* Robert *Brown!*"

"Oh, do stop shouting like that and repeating everything I tell you."

"But how do you *know*?"

"Oh, everyone knows by now. It's come out. I think
he left the marriage licence about or the woman went to
make a scene at his home or something. Anyway, it's a
fact. He's secretly married all the time. And he insulted
me proposing to me like that when he was married."
Cornelia's tears began to well again into her forget-me-
not blue eyes. "Oh, men are such *brutes*. First you—"

"Yes, darling . . . but what do you want me to do
about it?"

"I want you to go and *horsewhip* him."

"Y-yes," said Peter thoughtfully. "I would—I
honestly would—but I haven't got a horsewhip, and I
don't know anyone who has. And it hardly seems worth
while buying one just to use once, does it? I mean, it isn't
as if I had a horse and could get my money's worth out of
it."

"Oh, you are a *brute*. Doesn't your blood *boil* to think
I've been insulted?"

"Yes, it boils like anything, but—"

"If you won't horsewhip him, go and thrash him,
then."

"Y-yes," said Peter, still more thoughtfully. "Yes, that's quite a good idea, and I'd do it—honestly I would, darling—but we go to the same boxing class, and he can lick me hollow every time. Look here, darling, let's treat the fellow with the contempt he deserves. He's beneath our notice. Utterly beneath it. . . ."

The conversation ran on to its inevitable conclusion.

The other conversation was a little less dramatic but would still have interested Robert considerably.

Miss Amelia Blake and Miss Gregoria Mutch had gathered round Mr. Solomon at his garden gate. Mr. Solomon, an earnest and harassed-looking man, was the superintendent of the Sunday School. He was the type of man who is born to be superintendent of a Sunday School. The Sunday School bounded his mental horizon on all sides. Without it he would have wilted and died.

"You see, with the Vicar being away," Miss Amelia Blake was saying, "we felt that you were the person to come to. . . . After all, he used to go to the Sunday School when he was a little boy, didn't he?"

"Er—yes," agreed Mr. Solomon, his harassed expression deepening.

"Well, now that this dreadful thing's happened, we feel that you ought to go and break it to his parents. They know *nothing* about it."

"Er—are you sure?"

"Yes. . . . As a matter of fact we've just met Mrs. Brown, and quite obviously she knows nothing about it. We felt that it wasn't our place to tell her. . . .It's the dear Vicar's really, but as he's away we've come to you. We've thought it over very carefully, and we feel that it's your duty to break the news to the boy's poor parents. . . ."

Mr. Solomon, his harassed expression bordering on despair, ran his hands wildly through his hair, then automatically smoothed it down again because it was his rule always to try to set an example of personal tidiness to his charges.

"B-b-but are you *sure* about this secret marriage?" he said.

"Oh, *quite*," said Miss Gregoria Mutch firmly. "His younger brother happened to find a letter from the wife. Or something like that. Anyway, it's *absolutely* certain. Only his parents don't know."

"Why didn't the younger brother tell them?"

"Robert *terrorised* him into secrecy. Or something like that. Anyway, the boy found the proof, and his parents ought to be informed. *And* by you, Mr. Solomon, because we always look upon you as the dear Vicar's deputy. *And* as soon as possible. . . . "

"B-b-but really," stammered Mr. Solomon, "I-I-I really don't think I'm quite the right person. I—"

The conversation continued to its inevitable conclusion.

*   *   *

Three sets of people were walking down the road towards the Browns' house.

First went Robert in all innocence, unaware of the two personifications of Nemesis behind him. He wore his trilby hat and carried the bandbox containing Ermyntrude. Jameson had not been at home when he called for his trilby, so he had had to postpone the explanation.

Behind him came Mr. Solomon, accompanied by Miss Amelia Blake and Miss Gregoria Mutch.

Behind them came Cornelia Gerrard and Peter Greenham.

Both Mr. Solomon and Peter Greenham walked

slowly and as if reluctantly, evidently urged on by their companions.

"We won't come in, of course," Miss Amelia Blake was saying, "because, well, I don't think it would be very *nice* for ladies to be there, but we'll stay outside and wait for you. You can tell us all about it when you come out. You must ask to see the father alone first."

Mr. Solomon cast his mind about desperately. It was a dreadful position, but he saw no way out of it. One must do one's duty. Still—a horrible possibility struck him. Suppose the whole thing was a mare's nest. What a fool he'd look. He must find out first. . . . The boy had almost reached the gate.

He muttered "Excuse me," and set off at a run down the road. He caught up Robert just as he was lifting the latch and fixed him with a stern eye.

"Robert," he said "is this terrible thing I hear of you true?"

Robert's gaze faltered. So often in his childhood had Mr. Solomon faced him with that stern eye over some childish misdemeanour that his gaze even now faltered almost automatically on meeting Mr. Solomon's. He must have heard about Ermyntrude, of course. What a fuss people were making about that wretched hat.

"Yes," he muttered, then, remembering that he was nineteen and no longer attended Mr. Solomon's Sunday School, added with spirit: "but I don't see what business it is of yours."

"It *is* my business," said Mr. Solomon, and again the severity of his gaze made Robert feel and look as if he had been discovered eating bull's-eyes when it was his turn to say the collect. "It is the business of every decent man. Do your parents know about it?"

"No," admitted Robert, automatically making a movement with his mouth as if to conceal a bull's-eye and feeling rather surprised to find it empty.

Mr. Solomon pushed open the gate. "I'm coming in to see your parents, Robert," he said grimly.

Mr. and Mrs. Brown were sitting in the morning-room—Mr. Brown reading the newspaper, Mrs. Brown darning socks. They looked up in surprise when Mr. Solomon entered, followed by Robert—Mr. Solomon looking grave and portentous, Robert looking aggrieved and guilty, and holding a bandbox behind him as if trying to conceal it.

"I'm afraid that I have bad news for you," began Mr. Solomon.

"William's been run over," said Mrs. Brown tragically. "I knew it would happen. I've warned him over and over again."

Mr. Solomon reassured her on that point with a majestically upraised hand.

"No. Mrs. Brown. William is all right. As far as I know, that is. It's your other son who—"

At that moment Cornelia and Peter burst in unannounced. Or rather, Cornelia burst in dragging an obviously reluctant Peter.

"There he is," she said, pointing dramatically at Robert. She turned impatiently to Peter. "Well, aren't you going to *do* anything?"

Mr. Brown was gradually recovering from the paralysis of bewilderment that had held him speechless since the beginning of the scene.

"Will someone please tell me," he said politely, "what this is all about?"

Cornelia turned to him, stamping her foot with fury.

"Robert proposed to me this morning, and now I hear—"

"I *never* proposed to you," broke in Robert indignantly.

"*What?*" she screamed. "You deny that you proposed to me?"

"Certainly," said Robert.

"*Oh!*" She swung round on Peter. "And there you stand letting me be insulted over and over *again* before your very eyes. Can't you even knock him *down*?"

Mr. Solomon again raised his hand in a gravely imperious gesture.

"Leave this to me, Miss Gerrard," he said. He turned to Robert. "Hadn't you better make a clean breast of it, my boy? You know what I mean. . . . Where is she?"

"She's in here," said Robert sulkily, putting the bandbox down on the floor. He was *sick* of Ermyntrude. He'd never known such a fuss about a hat in his life before. . . . He'd jolly well never want to wear one again for the rest of his life. . . .

Mr. Solomon's expression grew sterner.

"Don't trifle with me, my boy," he began, but Mr. Brown had risen from his seat and made his way swiftly across the room to the door. He flung it open and dragged in William by an ear that had obviously just been applied to the keyhole.

"I thought I heard you there," he said. Then, still holding William's ear in an iron grip, he turned to the others.

"When anything utterly inexplicable happens in this house, I generally find that William can explain it. . . . Come on, young man, out with it!"

William had been listening to the scene in growing consternation, wondering how on earth he could extricate Robert from the morass into which he seemed to have led him. He now resigned himself to the inevitable. Sooner or later they'd get the whole story from him, so he might as well tell it to them. Only, as retribution surely awaited him at the end, he would make the tale as long as possible.

As far as his father's grip on his ear would allow him, he settled down to it. . . .

"Well," he said slowly, "it was like this. You see, it all began with the typewriter. . . ."

THE END

Richmal Crompton
William at War

In the dark days of the Second World War, everyone in
Britain must do their bit to help defeat the enemy.

William is determined to offer his services to his country –
whether it wants him or not. But to the Outlaws' surprise,
their enthusiastic contribution to the war effort is hardly
ever appreciated . . .

Here are ten hilarious stories about William – at war!

'Probably the funniest, toughest children's books ever
written.' *Sunday Times*